A Trial Lawyer's Journey

WARRIOR IN HIGH HEELS

JUDITH A. CORBIN

LUMINARE PRESS
WWW.LUMINAREPRESS.COM

Warrior in High Heels
Copyright © 2019 Judith A. Corbin

All rights reserved. This book or any portion thereof may not be reproduced or used in any manner whatsoever without the express written permission of the publisher, except for the use of brief quotations in a book review.

Printed in the United States of America

Cover Design: Melissa K. Thomas

Luminare Press
442 Charnelton
Eugene, OR 97401
www.luminarepress.com

LCCN: 2019910567
ISBN: 978-1-64388-057-0

This book is dedicated to Supreme Court Justice Ruth Bader Ginsburg, a noteworthy champion of women's rights. Appointed to the Supreme Court in 1993 by President Clinton, he saw beneath Ginsburg's reserved exterior, "a heroic American woman— to be sure—this is a woman with a big heart."

President Carter, who had appointed Ginsburg to the federal Court of Appeals, spoke of Ginsburg as "the most significant lawyer of the times, taking on women's rights cases one short step at a time in the pattern of Thurgood Marshall fighting for civil rights." Her astute intellect is widely recognized.

Justice Ginsburg's lifework means "fighting for the things you care about, which will lead others to join you." Ginsburg has been dubbed "The Fire and Steel on the Supreme Court." (Eleanor H. Ayer, in her book of the same name.) Numerous books and films have featured Ginsburg's life and accomplishments.

I first encountered Ruth Bader Ginsburg as the author of my law school casebook "Sex-Based Discrimination" in the 1970s. Her passionate lifelong journey of historical significance has inspired me ever since.

Table of Contents

Take One 1

First Shot: Firearms 7

Abomination and Maternal Madness 13

About Girls and Guns 25

Rape Case Gamble 33

About Boys 47

Pussy Prosecutor 55

Courtroom Fashionistas 65

Bank Robbery: Slam Dunk 73

Footfalls 81

Requiem for Rennie 89

Lawyer Wannabe 99

Red, White and Blue October 117

Sisterhood 123

Condemnations 131

Running After Rabbits 145

Token Woman 159

It's A Wrap 167

Psycho Sam 179

Cultural Lesson 195

Discrimination Hades 207

Roller Coaster Ride: Court of Appeals. 229

Author's Afterword
The Girl Left Behind: Leaving Footprints 247

Acknowledgements. 251

Chapter 1

Take One

I DIDN'T NEED THE ALARM THAT DECEMBER morning, after tossing and turning for hours before giving in and getting up. My husband's gentle snoring buzzed on. The shutter slats showed a typical Spokane grayish light outside, with a trace of snow in the fading moonlight. A slice of cold air sneaked in through the slit in the upraised window. I liked air in the bedroom at night.

I closed the bathroom door and began brushing my teeth. In my sleepy stupor, a fuzzy image of Jimmy Carter appeared in the depths of the mirror. Was I losing my mind? I blinked a few times, and gripped the edge of the sink to get back to brushing my teeth. Drank some water, closed my eyes and calmed myself.

I dressed in my carefully laid-out clothes for my first day. Downstairs in the kitchen, I forced myself to wash down a piece of honey toast with a cup of black coffee. It stuck in my throat and caused a coughing fit. My husband Michael padded into the kitchen looking sleepy and puzzled.

"You're all dressed and ready, isn't it too early?"

"Couldn't sleep, just…." I started coughing again.

He kissed my cheek. "You'll do fine, Diana, everything will be just fine…."

I managed a small smile, feeling restless to get going.

Driving downtown, my gloved hands gripped the wheel as if to fend off demons. Why am I so nervous? I'm 38 years old with three kids, our older daughter already married at 18, a rebel like me. I'd been around the block, eventually changed my tune, then conquered college and law school. Just breathe, I told myself.

The morning light brightened as I parked my car in a street lot, then walked to the rhythm of my clicking heels on the sidewalk toward the U.S. Courthouse.

I marched up the entry stairs of the nine-story federal building dressed in a steel gray tweed suit, my hands brandishing an empty black briefcase like a shield, while my lungs gulped for oxygen. Inside the heavy courthouse door, no electronic security machines blocked the hallway like they do these days. I spotted only a bulky U.S. Marshall smoking a cigarette as he leaned against the cement side wall facing the door.

Reaching the eighth floor, one of my black high-heeled pumps caught on the elevator edge. I yanked the heel free, lifted my shoulders, and plunged straight ahead to the receptionist's desk.

"I'm Diana Keatts, the new Assistant United States Attorney."

After giving me a quick once-over, the receptionist led me down a hallway maze to a corner office furnished with looming bookcases. Opposite the door, an American flag and framed photograph of current President Jimmy Carter caught my attention. James Wilson sat in a lazy pose wearing an open-collar shirt and khaki pants in the fold of a huge L-shaped desk. At a small conference table, several men in serious dark suits and ties looked up from coffee cups and yellow legal pads. On side chairs, a few women sat with steno notebooks and curious glances.

I already knew James Wilson, the United States Attorney for the Eastern District of Washington, a political appointee, who had hired me. He jumped up and shook my hand. With introductions all around, I learned the names of the Assistant United States Attorneys, "AUSAs" as they were called, and the names of the legal secretaries. I concentrated on names and faces, wishing for nametags, especially since the men all had the same dark-suit-white-shirt-and-tie look. Someone pulled out a chair for me at the table.

James announced the Pledge of Allegiance. Everyone stood, facing the flag in the corner. I copied the others, placing my right hand on my heart as James began, "I pledge allegiance to the flag...."

After an abrupt pause and silence, I heard snickering. James and a few of the men bent over with loud guffaws and turned to me. James snorted. His gray eyes crinkled with unreadable mirth. My open mouth morphed into a forced smile. A hot blush unrolled across my stunned face as I struggled to comprehend. Dissing the flag and the Pledge of Allegiance? Was my anxious mind playing tricks? I looked around and swallowed hard, full of confused shock and embarrassment. I didn't get it.

My brand-new lawyer bravado told me to follow their lead and not make a mistake. I'd been investigated, fingerprinted and granted a security clearance for the privilege of joining the Department of Justice. I wasn't going to screw it up on the first day, so arranged my face into a neutral expression.

But my brain ran in a loop puzzling about the joke—or was it? Why? Part of an initiation? No one explained the strangeness.

After the attorneys and staff in this federal enclave settled down, one or two clapped me on the back gingerly as we sat down to business. No one else seemed upset. I scanned the room as though nothing unusual had happened. My head and heart were racing—was this serious, or a candid camera moment? Were they all subversives? Or insane?

Unspoken subtext prickled my skin and my eyes blinked too much. Someone put a cup of coffee in front of me. "Cream?"

I struggled to assume a lawyer's mask, while my body temperature cooled down. I picked up a pen and legal pad to make notes of discussion about pending cases, and forced myself to concentrate over the rapid tingling in my ears. Nothing was legible. I glanced up once and caught a flash of the flag, next to the photograph of Jimmy Carter.

In my mind, the first day's meeting lasted for hours. James leaned back in his chair, feet on the oversize desk, as the AUSAs droned on. My hand pushed my pen as fast as I could write, filling the yellow pages with scribbled trial schedules, status reports and names of judges.

The secretaries eyed me with covert curiosity I could feel. While answering the men's questions about status and schedules, they added extra details. The secretaries' eyes chilled me, adding to my sense of not belonging. I could feel sizing-up going on, although I had no thought of my future role as one of their bosses. My ice-cold hand gripped my coffee cup as I listened.

The chief criminal deputy, Jay Colter, mentioned a firearms case.

"Going to trial on Wednesday. Should be one day, in the Yakima courthouse. ATF case."

James took his feet off the desk and leaned forward. "How about Diana sitting in? She can learn the ins and outs of firearms cases."

Jay paused a moment, then looked over at me. "Okay, sure."

I nodded.

After that, I lost track of the meeting. My mind spun out of control with the need to prepare for my first official federal courtroom appearance. All I knew was that ATF stood for the Alcohol, Tobacco and Firearms federal agency. I wanted to ask, "Are you sure I should do this so soon?"

When I got home that night, Michael and our two teenage kids still at home wanted details. It was hard to tell about the flag incident. The kids thought it funny. Michael didn't.

Later in the bedroom, he blurted out his take on the flag deal.

"They're trying to fuck with you. Maybe some sort of first-day joke, or they're frustrated feds looking for amusement. James, he sounds like a real wild card."

I tried to forget my confused embarrassment. Find some comfort in sleep. It didn't happen.

Chapter 2

First Shot: Firearms

THE NEXT DAY WAS A QUICK LESSON ABOUT ATF's enforcement of illegal gun possession. The defendant was caught with automatic weapons in his Yakima home in central Washington. Civilian possession of "machine guns" violated federal law back in 1977. Based upon credible information, the ATF obtained a warrant, searched the defendant's home, and seized the guns hidden under the defendant's living room couch.

AUSA Jay Colter was a slim, hyper kind of guy, who talked and reacted fast, laughed freely, and chain smoked by the looks of the huge ashtray of cigarette butts on his desk. We prepared for the criminal trial in Jay's office. I listened intently while Cliff, an ATF agent, reviewed the firearms case for my benefit.

Cliff was a tall, 30-ish macho guy with rough edges and steady grey eyes, who ran through details of the search warrant, arrest and evidence. Hard facts, no frills. Jay and Cliff made offside comments I didn't get about why the defendant's attorney wouldn't plead his client guilty. Just focus on the facts, I told myself.

Jay took scant notes. I wrote down every detail. Then out of the blue, Jay told Cliff I'd be handling his direct examination at trial. Jay looked at me. I sucked in my breath.

"Cliff can rattle off the details of his report in his sleep. No problem. All you need to do is follow the info in the report. Cliff will explain it all to the jury."

"Uh, okay." I felt uneasy and excited all at once.

I reviewed every piece of paper in the investigative file, the federal statues, including Jay's trial brief, the jury instructions, and whatever else I could find to help me. I checked back with a few questions for Jay. He breezily made explanations, then looked at me as though he had an idea.

"Diana, I think you could do the opening statement for the case. It's not that hard—this is a simple case of firearms possession. You merely need to outline the evidence to show what we'll prove to the jury. Basically, the elements of the statute."

"Jay, uh, I could do it, but you'll have to check over my notes before trial." I felt a lump in my throat.

"It's the easiest part of the case, given at the start of a trial when the jury will be paying close attention to the ABCs of what we'll show through witnesses and evidence."

Jay made it sound so simple. Not much sleep for me again that night.

The next afternoon Jay and I flew over to Yakima in central Washington on a small Cascade Airways plane that wrenched my queasy stomach with its bumpy ride. We checked into a nondescript motel near the federal courthouse.

That evening we met with ATF agent Cliff at a nearby sports bar. Jay and Cliff relaxed while they rehashed past cases, told a few raunchy jokes and threw down drinks. My fearful stomach churned, as I sipped my bourbon and water, trying to act calm. I hadn't thought to bring my pink stomach tabs.

We finally went over the agent's testimony as I marked up a few revisions to my detailed outline. Cliff knew his stuff. Jay offered me a cigarette. It tasted good after ten years without.

Back in my motel room, I curled up under the bedspread to stop my shivering. I re-read my notes till after midnight. I awoke with a start at 4:00 a.m. Got up, tried a few tough facial expressions in the bathroom mirror until I burst out laughing. That helped.

I hardly remember the trial itself, but I pushed myself to the limit. Jay remained his laid-back self, overlaid with a tough-guy serious edge for the jury's benefit. Possession of illegal firearms was small potatoes in the federal scheme of offenses, but this first real trial was do or die for me.

The jury took exactly one hour to convict the defendant. I reacted with a cold rush or hot flash—I couldn't tell which.

"Wow, we won!" I said when we got out of earshot of the courtroom. I could hardly keep from skipping in my high heels. I could get addicted to this.

"Yeah, now you have a conviction—a notch in your belt. You'll get used to the routine."

Notches in my belt established "cred" with federal agents, as I later came to understand. The agents expected guilty verdicts at trial for their hard-worked cases, not AUSA's "declinations to prosecute," or worse, courtroom verdicts of Not Guilty. I needed to demonstrate toughness and trial success to convince them to work with me, the brand-new lone female federal prosecutor in the office.

I learned about various categories of guns in the course of the firearms case. When preparing for the trial in Jay's office, he explained differences between hand guns and the illegal ones seized by the ATF. He pulled out his own pistol and showed it to me.

"I carry it for protection, basically in case of emergency. You probably heard about the federal prosecutor who was shot a few months ago in Texas."

I felt intimidated by the pistol resting on his desk, but sat there as he explained how it worked. Then he put it back into the holster under his suit jacket and changed the subject.

This got me wondering about the possibility of personal threats or violence, something I hadn't thought about because I was so taken with the idealized role of a prosecutor. This conversation with Jay threw me into a temporary tailspin, worrying about whether I should carry a gun. I couldn't really picture myself going that far. Thoughts ran back and forth, and I even had some dreams about guns. Running away from a gun pointing at me, searching for a gun and not finding it, all jumbled together. I would awaken in a sweat. My solution—repress these unwelcome thoughts. I had important work to do.

That first whirlwind week brought me back to a

stack of files on my desk that shouted out to me when I returned to the office from the Yakima firearms trial. As I pushed through review of the criminal cases, I often dropped by Jay's office next door to ask questions and get his opinions. When he joked with the agents who hung around his office using the "f" word as frequent punctuation, I acted blasé. I couldn't waste time obsessing about the agents' coarse language, as the files required me to carefully focus on the merits of each case in this new world of federal prosecutors.

I had no idea of the breadth of federal criminal jurisdiction, but I would soon find out.

Chapter 3

Abomination and Maternal Madness

I REALIZED THAT WEARING A GENERIC BUSINESS suit like the men didn't identify me as a lawyer in the 1970s. Nor did it give me routine credibility. My panty-hosed legs and high heels below my skirt hem emphasized my femaleness, as pantsuits hadn't caught on yet. I ignored federal agents' noticeable puzzlement over my unique role as a woman federal prosecutor. I postured around, trying to appear tough and gutsy.

With arraignments, preliminary hearings and unfamiliar motions, I charged into the fray with untested edginess. My excessive research helped to double check myself. When colleagues made flip comments, I closed my lips to prevent quick retorts that sprang into my head. After all, I hadn't sweated my way through law school to sit on the sidelines. I looked straight ahead with fanatical determination, and continued smoking now and then.

Within the first year, my defiant prosecutor exterior and my repressed feminine instincts bumped up against each other. One morning I brought See's chocolates to the office to celebrate news of my first grandchild's birth, the baby boy of my older daughter. I sat down in the coffee break room, as my excitement warmed up the female staff. We savored chocolates and coffee, chatting amiably about baby stuff. That lasted for about five minutes.

In the hallway, I overheard AUSA Karl Gray talking to someone as they walked toward the break room.

"You can meet our new girl, she'll handle the sex cases now," Karl's distinctive booming voice announced. I had yet to work with Karl, who was the Chief Deputy to James.

What girl, what sex cases? In a split second, I realized he meant me. My adrenalin spiked.

"Diana, this is Charlie Emerson, the FBI agent who handles reservation cases," said Karl.

Charlie, a tall agent with a short haircut and sober expression, shook hands with me. I stammered a hello. We disappeared into my nearby office. I took a deep breath and closed the door. He was friendly but reserved, as we checked each other out. I noticed his steady hands and orderly file.

After a few get-acquainted preliminaries, he explained that he had a case to present for prosecution. His expression changed from businesslike to deadly grim.

"Diana, this is a shocking case. A gruesome rape of a three-old Indian boy on a nearby reservation."

"What? Why is this our case? Sounds like something the state would handle."

"We have federal jurisdiction under the "Major Crimes Act. The tribe handles misdemeanors and tribal matters, but major crimes like murder, rape, assault, are on us."

My heart raced. Prosecute a crime for a sadistic sexual assault of a child? I wasn't ready for this.

Emerson told me that the boy's mother, Ayla, had left her son Joey with a 21-year-old cousin, Eneas, while Ayla went out partying with her friends. Eneas, a rebellious alcoholic loner, had a juvenile record of minor offenses on the reservation policed by the Bureau of Indian Affairs.

Charlie went on reading from his report.

"The mother returned the next morning to pick up her son. Three-year-old Joey fussed and clung to her. In his high chair at home he threw his crackers and cheese on the floor, refusing to eat. When she tried to change his diaper to put him down for a nap, Joey screamed and fought. Ayla noticed blood on his diaper. She tried to clean him and put on a new diaper—he kept screaming."

I felt dizzy. I could hardly listen to this.

As he howled, Ayla began to suspect what he meant in his halting baby gibberish. Her concern turned to horror, Charlie related.

"E-e-en-tutu-my butt, Joey sobbed over and over.

"While Ayla hugged and rocked her whimpering son, he fell into a fitful sleep. Ayla laid on the couch with Joey not knowing what do to. She finally called her mother, who drove over from Idaho. They bundled Joey up in a blanket and drove to an off-reservation medical clinic about 20 miles away.

"Pediatrician Dr. Robert Murphy's findings upon examination revealed abrasions, redness and swelling in the child's anus and rectum. He confirmed to the traumatized mother that the boy's injuries were consistent with sodomy. Dr. Murphy reported these conclusions to the local Bureau of Indian Affairs agent who contacted the FBI."

By then I was speechless.

Listening to agent Emerson's halting recital of the ghastly facts, the taste of vomit rose in my throat. I fought to remain calm, but my hand shook out of control as I wrote notes. Leaden feelings weighed me down as I wrote out the script of a real-life horror film. I gulped down my disgust and disbelief, feeling totally inadequate. I sat at my desk motionless after Charlie Emerson left my office. Then re-read the FBI report and felt sick again. I wanted a cigarette.

I don't know how long I sat frozen at my desk before I had the courage to tell my boss James what I had just learned from the agent. I had to discuss it with him, of course. After James slowly read the FBI report and medical records, he took a deep breath and shook his head. I hadn't seen him sit so still before. Finally, he sighed and then spoke in a monotone.

"Diana, get going and research the statutes. Review the options for prosecution. Then get back to me."

"Okay." I could see the shock in his eyes.

That afternoon I spent hours in our law library searching out rape law as defined by the unique statues governing crimes on the Indian reservation. Initially stymied because the facts did not fall within the statutes, I pored over the books until my vision was blurry. Finally found a possible way to charge the defendant. James came in and sat down next to me amid the books scattered over the long library table. I told him what I had found and not found. He nodded as he told me to write up my research findings. Tedious case law research in the 1970s took a long time. That was before we could spin out legal research on a computer. I worked into the evening.

When I finally got home that night, I jolted Michael with details of the child rape case.

His first question, "Why you? Why do you have to handle this miserable case?"

"Jay and James gave me no choice. It's just…just do it."

"That's unfair. You're the newest one in the office."

"I guess they didn't want to do it."

"Well, yeah, who would?"

I changed the subject to talk about our daughter and new grandson, although the gloom of the case lingered over us.

The next day, I accompanied agent Emerson to the reservation in a dry desolate area of northeast Washington about an hour's drive from Spokane. We met Ayla at the door of her small unpainted house. Anger gripped her face like a vise, showing puffy eyes and lack of sleep. Joey's dark eyes in an elfin face peeked out from behind his mother, his little fist holding a fold of her long, wrinkled skirt. He looked younger than three. A grey-muzzled black dog sniffed air and stood firm between Joey and us.

"Sit down, Black. Sit." Ayla said, as she pushed the dog over next to Joey. We sat down at the kitchen table.

That painful interview was brief, as Ayla's mumbled

responses were slow and inarticulate. She managed a small grateful look as we left. I felt so sorry for her and her baby son, I could hardly keep the tears from rolling down my cheeks on the drive back to Spokane with Charlie.

After the FBI investigation, I charged the defendant with the federal crime of "Assault Resulting in Serious Bodily Injury." This peculiar charge turned out to be the only prosecutorial option because the Major Crimes Act omitted sodomy in the definition of rape. Jay, the chief criminal deputy, helped me frame the criminal assault complaint. I called the assault the child rape case from then on. Jay knew I was unsure of myself handling such a bizarre case. But no doubt he was relieved that the case wasn't his.

"I'm so freaked about having to present these facts in open court," I said.

"Diana, the defense attorney won't want to go to trial. The defendant will probably plead. Just be patient, it will work out," Jay assured me.

The case did not plead out. By the time it went to trial, it was totally *my* case and a huge responsibility. I was armed with facts, legal briefs and prosecutorial vengeance. Defense attorney Roger Alberg and I skirmished before trial about admissibility of the insanity defense he'd raised at the last moment. When the U.S. District Court judge allowed it, that meant I needed to hire a psychiatrist to examine the defendant and testify for the prosecution. Then another pretrial issue came up.

The evidence rules prohibited the three-year-old victim from testifying in court because of his age. His few baby words to his mother about the sexual penetration could not be repeated by the mother because it was inadmissible hearsay. This was crucial evidence and needed to be heard by the jury.

In a preliminary hearing, I argued that the boy's words should be admissible as "excited utterance" testimony, an exception to the hearsay rule. To my relief, the judge ruled that the mother could testify about her son's words because they were spoken almost immediately after the incident, and the child was not legally capable of lying. Thus, the words were credible admissible evidence. To hear the fragile boy's imperfect words identifying his attacker would surely horrify the jury. I was counting on that.

Over my objections, the judge also ruled that little Joey should not be present in court—too inflammatory. Ayla flared up with anger when I told her that.

The trial began with jury selection and opening statements. When Ayla was called from the hallway to testify, she paused at the door of the courtroom in full view of the jury and handed Joey carefully to his grandmother who then backed up slowly into the hallway. Ayla walked ahead to the witness chair to be sworn in. I sucked in my breath, detecting a shuffle of feet at the defense table, expecting an objection and the judge's wrath. Ayla had violated the judge's order and my instructions to her that Joey could not be present in the courtroom.

I heard only my loud heartbeat. I knew that I—or at least Ayla—had gotten away with it. She wanted the jury to see her vulnerable baby son, so she acted on her own without informing me. She was cagier than I thought. I had just escaped my first encounter with a viable contempt citation or possible grounds for appeal. I looked down at my notes.

On the witness stand, Ayla sobbed as she repeated the graphic words of her child, as well as her explanation that the boy's word "tutu" meant penis. She told how her son knew the defendant as "E-e-en," his baby way of saying Eneas. Anger and hurt hooded Ayla's eyes. She survived the direct testimony and minimal cross-examination with surprising inner strength. Her authenticity and sincerity overshadowed her hesitations. The jurors leaned forward in their seats.

The defendant looked small next to his beefy lawyer. His dark hair kept falling over his downturned face. I could hardly look at him.

Dr. Robert Murphy's testimony demanded respect, as his outrage was evident through the graphic medical terms. As a local family practitioner and pediatrician, this had to be unusual duty for him. The explicit medical records were admitted as documentary evidence. The jurors would read them in the jury room when they deliberated.

The prosecution case unfolded according to plan, even with my boss James breathing down my neck at the prosecutor's table during the entire trial. He had informed me the day before trial of his decision to sit as co-counsel. His stubborn obsessions about the trial outcome, the press coverage and especially my inexperience made me crazy. He handed me scribbled notes and fidgeted. I swallowed my impatience and distraction in the presence of his long shadow.

James rarely tried cases himself, but was good at giving lots of advice. I didn't talk back. But even as a beginner, I reacted at trial with my own strategy and instincts. I ignored his sighs.

At breaks in the prosecutor's room, James and I rushed to light up so we could smoke two cigarettes in a 15-minute recess. He could burn one cigarette halfway down in a single inhale. James didn't carry cigarettes because his wife and his cardiologist had cut off his unhealthy habit. He borrowed from me. Now that I had a supply in my purse, I counted as one of the guys when it came to bumming cigarettes.

As we sucked our smokes down, James said, "You have to ask the doctor another question."

"I already finished his direct."

"Uh…you need to establish that the child's anus could physically admit an adult male's erect penis." He looked away, and took another drag from the cigarette.

"What? Why? I don't need to. The doctor already said it was sodomy."

"Doesn't matter—you need to ask the question."

"But he already described the injuries."

"I'm telling you that the question must be asked and answered."

"I don't see why."

"The jurors might wonder about it. Quit being so delicate. We need to slam the jurors with the gory details. That's it."

"I already did that."

"You *will* ask the question. Get on with it. Let's go."

I choked on the smoke and smashed out the butt. Smelling of tension and cigarettes, we traipsed back into court. I recalled the doctor to the stand who replied "yes" to the question. The jurors squirmed. So did I.

Now the defense had its turn. Their psychiatrist witness testified that the defendant's alcoholism supported the insanity defense, as well as "limited capacity." I followed with rebuttal testimony by our prosecution psychiatrist. I worried this might confuse the jury, even though the jury would receive specific definitions of the defenses of insanity and limited capacity in the documents taken to the jury room.

After closing arguments and recital of jury instructions by the judge, the bailiff led the jury into the conference room for deliberations. A local reporter hung around the courthouse, hoping for a quick verdict.

Back in my office on the eighth floor below the courtroom, I felt a spike of satisfaction at doing the best job I could, especially my opening statement and closing argument. I worried about my awkward cross examination of the slick defense psychiatrist. After the trial, James didn't have much to say. I didn't either. The only thing to do was wait for the jury's verdict.

The next day, "Guilty" filled up the courtroom. The judge thanked and dismissed the jury, and the bailiff announced, "All rise."

Dark silence hung in the air for a split second. Suddenly the defendant wailed, his voice an eerie primordial lament of pain. Echoes resonated from the high courtroom ceiling. I flinched. My ears rang and my jaw went slack.

The U.S. marshals jumped up and whisked the defendant away. The judge, the press and silent observers filed out of the still courtroom. Drained and weak, I scooped up my legal pad and files, dashed into the hallway and fled down the stairs to my office. I passed the reporters cornering my boss. When I reached safe haven, I collapsed against my closed office door.

Tears crowded my eyes, and I hobbled to my desk, dropped my head and shook. The weight of grief washed over me. The mother and the child. The echoes of the wailing defendant. I couldn't sort it out in my exhaustion.

Slumped on my messy desk, I felt mixed relief because the proud satisfaction of winning a case was murky. The child rape case didn't stack up as a win for anyone. A just verdict would not heal the losers. I couldn't compose my conflicted self.

After my somber reflections while hiding in my office, and a few "congrats" from colleagues after the jury's guilty verdict, I drove home in a blur of fatigue, my head full of images of the victims.

I had a change of scene as I drove up, seeing my older daughter's car in our driveway. In the kitchen, she cradled her three-month-old son, Brandon. My busy trial schedule hadn't given me much time with my new grandson. I reached for him and nuzzled his velvet babyness. He wiggled and giggled. We laughed and melted with his sweetness.

After they left, I remembered the joy when I brought chocolates to my office to celebrate Brandon's birth, which seemed so long ago. My warm family connections helped me feel maternal gratitude, helping to shut down my battlefield persona. But not for long.

A few months later, I argued the criminal appeal of the child rape case at the Ninth Circuit Court of Appeals, which affirmed the District Court's rulings. The appeal rekindled circles of storm clouds. I couldn't forget the actual trial with Joey's dark elfin eyes, Ayla's rage, and the defendant's primitive tribal wailing at the verdict.

I still stung from James' interference, and his "told you so" attitude after the child rape trial. His bossy control hampered my evolving confidence. James' go-to instruction was "be tough to the nth degree and get convictions," while he often acted out his confusing sporadic criticism and back-handed encouragement.

Emphasizing my tough objective role to bring cases to a just verdict didn't erase my subverted feelings. But too much feeling interfered, so I became good at repression. I went to the gym and took walks by myself. In the evenings Michael and I talked about plans for future vacations and maybe remodeling our house. By then we were drinking way more wine than usual before dinner. Hard to sort it all out.

Chapter 4

About Girls and Guns

I CRAVED TO WORK ON ANY CASE WITH AGENTS OR AUSAs to learn the ropes. When Karl Gray asked me to help him prepare a tax evasion case for trial, I jumped right in.

Karl, the senior deputy AUSA, a heavy set, outgoing guy in his late 50s with youthful light brown hair, seemed pleasant enough. He'd been in the U.S. Attorney's office forever, through presidential appointees of both political stripes. I imagined the current appointee, James Wilson, confounded him, but Karl went along with James and his quirks. We didn't talk politics in the office because the Hatch Act prohibited government employees from engaging in political activities. I suspected Karl leaned toward the conservative side.

Karl no doubt took a deep breath when wild card democratic activist James Wilson was appointed by President Carter. Then James hired me, a complete unknown, politically and otherwise, right out of law school with no experience. I wondered to myself about possible unwritten hiring guidelines in President Carter's Department of Justice (DOJ), maybe giving some unspoken preference to female new hires. But of course, this was not an appropriate topic of political discussion in the office, so I never brought up my curiosity about the reasons for my hiring.

Karl's expertise in white collar crime often meant tax cases. Tax evasions presented exceptional evidentiary challenges. A chance to work with Karl would be a learning experience, as I knew nothing about these high-profile prosecutions. I imagined that James had pressed Karl to include me in the tax case, as he'd never seemed interested in working with me before.

I wanted to impress Karl. We began our hours together in his office sifting through files, the defendant's tax records and assets, investigative reports and case law.

One afternoon as the tax evasion trial date drew near, Karl and I sat at his office table sorting out trial exhibits. The process required organization of a huge number of documents to be admitted as evidence at trial, and sent to the jury room during deliberations. Proof was circumstantial, as we had no explicit evidence or direct witness testimony to nail the defendant with the crime. This cumulative "net worth" evidence was expected to show the defendant's lavish lifestyle and enormous assets as one avenue to convince the jury. Not an easy task.

While we worked, Karl mentioned his recent conversations with a DOJ lawyer and an IRS lawyer, both of whom furnished back-up trial support as well as briefs from similar prosecutions. Karl called them "the girl lawyers in D.C."

"Do you get good advice from those girl lawyers in D.C.?" I said.

"Yup."

"Sounds like they know their stuff."

"Yeah. It happens all the time now—whenever I call for help or approvals, I get the girls."

"You mean it wasn't always that way?"

"Nope," Karl sighed. "I've been a prosecutor for almost 20 years. All of a sudden there's a flood of them in D.C. Almost every time I call, I get a new girl on the phone."

He raised his eyebrows and frowned.

"Where did all the *boy* lawyers go?" I almost blurted out. I figured they were the bosses.

Karl looked away and shook his head. I kept going.

"Oh, you probably don't mind talking to all those girl lawyers."

"Uh, well, they don't give me trouble They're usually pretty sharp…"

"Sounds like they're taking over."

Then I looked down, having said enough. Maybe too much.

Inwardly, I wanted to cheer for the D.C. "girls" and shout out, it's about time for the women lawyers to take over. I hoped in D.C. they had role models and mentoring—more than in Spokane.

Karl shifted in his chair, his annoyance melting into pretrial jitters. That was contagious. Back to our trial prep. I flipped through the documents and our trial exhibit list while Karl marked up the trial brief. We concentrated on our work and said little else. I eyed him covertly—I think I could outsmart him if I needed to. But that errant thought wasn't productive.

The tax evasion case ended on the first day of trial when the defendant pled guilty to two counts in the indictment. Case closed, but not with Karl and me.

I was sure Karl realized I was chiding him during our work together. My needling was obvious. But his frequent references to "girl" lawyers bothered me. I felt that keenly. He wasn't mean or cruel. Maybe bewildered. I knew hiring me was not his idea.

The scarcity of women in law school graduates in eastern Washington made us invisible. Our appearance on the male-dominated scene created agitation—an unwelcome intrusion into their exclusive fraternity. As I think back to Karl's comments about the influx of women professionals into the Department of Justice in D.C., I recognize his ownership attitude—why are all these girl lawyers trespassing on my domain? Why do I have to ask legal advice and approval from girls no older than my daughters?

I didn't have the courage or time to start a serious conversation with him about his attitude and my agitation. I kept my distance and smart comebacks to myself—an issue of self-preservation.

As time passed, I felt that he listened more seriously to my ideas, noticed my long hours and appreciated my successes in court. But Karl continued to blurt out "the new girl lawyer in the office" when introducing me. Maybe he spoke those words about me as a showpiece, something to be noticed, I don't know. I should have told him to stop it.

Flat out antagonism by me against any of my AUSA colleagues would be risky. To whine, criticize or complain would only make things worse. Especially since I was making progress with my confident prosecution of courtroom cases. My warrior persona kicked in with ferocity to succeed. Winning was everything to me—it had been my history—in all levels of school, on the playground, in games and sports, and life in general. As a lawyer, I acted tough because that's what my male role models did. I desperately wanted to be in the game without criticism or limitations.

As months went by, Karl used the label "girl lawyer" less often. I detected a slight twinkle as if it was a joke, baiting me. That was after one time I finally blurted out "boy lawyers" in an offhand comment, not labeling him specifically of course. Karl and I tiptoed around with teasing barbs, not in front of others. One day I had a crazy idea to tape a copy of my birth certificate on the outside of my office door, just to document that I had long ago passed the girl stage. No one noticed, except some staff who laughed about it.

At times the invisible chip on my shoulder came loose or the mask I wore to avoid confrontation slipped. I'd look up with a start or make an offhand comment. My frequent self-talk told me that the guys' annoying behavior wasn't really that offensive. It was obvious that they were perplexed about my working as a prosecutor and wanted to know why. They needed *an explanation*. Similar to the dreaded question in employment interviews, "why would *you* want to become a lawyer?" Their comments may have come from an authentic struggle to understand changing perceptions of traditional male/female roles. But how could I explain my feelings of frustration to them when I couldn't figure them out myself?

My lack of clarity somehow seemed connected to my inward fears about potential risks of harm to me as a federal prosecutor. I had scary dreams of running, running, trying to get away or defend myself. Searching for a gun. Never finding one. Waking up with a start, my heart racing. Did this erupt from my first case about the illegal firearms and Jay's display of his pistol?

My husband Michael never wanted guns in the house. He'd used them for hunting as a boy, but told me he hated guns. I didn't want one in the house either. My parents didn't have guns.

In spite of all this, I started to think about carrying a gun. All the federal law enforcement officers had them, as well as Jay, my fellow prosecutor. Jack and some law school friends carried guns. Jack once asked me to go out for target practice at a gun range. I said no. I'd never touched a gun.

He persisted, "You should try it out, Diana. It's a great feeling."

Now I thought more about it. My large purse was full of stuff like a big wallet, cosmetics, a notebook, extra pantyhose in case of a run. I could hide a small gun under all that. Maybe this was the time.

I called Jack.

"I've decided to maybe get a gun."

"Really?"

"Yeah, I know this sounds crazy, but I want to look

at small hand guns. How about going to the gun shop with me?"

"Wow, Diana. That's a change of heart. What happened?"

"Nothing. I just want it for security. Protection, I guess."

"Okay."

"I'm imagining bad scenes with some of the violent crimes I'm prosecuting. I had a terrible dream last night, woke up in a cold sweat. Today I imagined owning a gun, you know, like you…"

"Yeah, I get that. You're not alone."

"I'll feel safer, maybe, packing heat."

Jack laughed, "So you finally want me to show you the ropes about guns?"

"Yeah. Listen, Jack, I don't want Michael to know. He'd raise holy hell. I'll just have to lie to him if it comes up."

Jack and I went to a local gun shop. After looking at the inventory of small firearms, I picked out a stainless-steel mini revolver with a pearl handle. I liked the looks of it. Jack took me out to the range a few times during the middle of the day during our work week, furtive trips with his gun and mine, which he was holding for me till I got good at handling it. I felt smug about our little gun trips, like I was getting away with something.

The pearl handle grip fit my hand, and I shot at the target until I got the feel. It was exciting when I finally hit that elusive target. We'd go out to the range on our lunch breaks now and then, just for the practice.

Jack showed me how to load, set the safety and best practices for handling guns. I started carrying the mini revolver in my purse, or under my car seat if I was going into the courthouse. I'd take my gun to depositions, out-of-town trips, and always when I was out at night by myself. I rarely left home without it.

At first, the gun made me feel anxious, the awful fear of having to use it. But over time I grew confident and a bit giddy When my hand touched the gun at the bottom of my purse, it made me feel shielded and safe. The little pearl-handled gun was my buddy, my protector.

When I did have it at home, the gun and extra ammo rested in the bottom of my second underwear drawer, under slips and frilly panties I rarely wore. I felt good having it there, and took the gun out sometimes when no one was home, just to look at its shiny handle. I was invincible.

Was I totally losing it? I'd always been a peacenik at heart. Was this all about my scary nightmares? What if the gun actually went off and hurt someone?

I pushed the worries out of my head, and didn't care about not telling Michael. I was a "girl" with a gun and nobody better mess with me. My altered state of fear disappeared, pushed aside with confidence, maybe false confidence, and didn't faze me any longer. I stopped having nightmares about guns.

Chapter 5

Rape Case Gamble

In the Eastern District of Washington, individual prosecutors gravitated toward specific federal agents they hung out with. Or maybe the guys preferred certain types of cases. For example, Karl worked white collar crimes with his buddies in the FBI and IRS. Jay prosecuted bank robberies, drug cases, firearms, the violent crimes. He liked to joke around with DEA, ATF and FBI agents about the dark details of crimes by seedy criminal derelicts and "fucking losers." Another AUSA handled complex condemnations and water law. These case preferences weren't exclusive, since our office had few AUSAs but covered all of Washington state east of the Cascade mountains, with satellite courthouses in Yakima and Richland.

I found myself all over the map in assignments, as James was expansive in educating me while I learned the ropes. But no one wanted the violent sexual assault crimes, which were termed the sex cases, so they came to me.

After the child rape case had been put away on appeal, another case came up on the Kalispell reservation within our jurisdiction. The victim was a single mother assaulted at night in her home. The attacker entered the dark house, and grabbed the victim while she was sleeping on the couch. Marty, a tribal member, couldn't see the assailant's face because of the darkness.

"Don't scream or I'll fucking kill you." The rapist held his hand over her mouth until Marty stopped struggling. "Hold still, or I'll kill you. Don't yell. Don't you dare yell."

Her two toddler children in the back bedroom slept through the attack.

Battered and bruised, she reported the rape to the agent at the Bureau of Indian Affairs (BIA). The agent sent her to the hospital to be examined. Findings were consistent with rape. After the BIA agent contacted him, FBI agent Charlie Emerson recorded Marty's statement which listed the perpetrator as "Unknown." Charlie questioned her about recent activities and boyfriends. She mentioned people she had been drinking with earlier in the evening. Marty's fearful looks overshadowed her tentative answers. Charlie repeatedly asked her if she suspected her attacker's identity. She stuttered, backed away, and said she couldn't see who he was.

Charlie questioned a few of Marty's friends, but leads went nowhere. He had a crime but no suspect.

Charlie called me about the case and said he was bringing the victim to my office. Disheveled and anxious, dark-haired Marty shuffled into the office but wouldn't look at me. She trembled on the edge of the chair in worn out jeans and a tight sweater that was unraveling, obviously distrustful and suspicious. I asked a few neutral questions. Asked about her children. That didn't change her demeanor. She looked at the floor and twisted her worn purse strap. She wanted out. I puzzled about what to do. I decided to ask Charlie to step outside my office for a moment. He reluctantly left and closed the door.

I sat down and re-read the investigative report while Marty sat there in a heap, shifting her scuffed boots around. I took a deep breath and looked up.

"Who was he?"

Nothing. She looked away.

"Did you know him?"

"I couldn't see nothing—too dark" she mumbled. "I gotta pick up my kids." She turned to stand up.

"Your children were asleep in their room?"

"He never hurt the kids."

"Was there anything—anything—that made you suspect who he was?"

She started for the door.

"Who was he?"

"No. No. I was drinking, maybe passed out. I don't know nothing about him. He was…so rough." She rubbed the back of her hand over her wet cheek.

"Nothing at all? There must have been something," I said.

"No. No. I said NO."

I stood up, tried to look her in the eyes.

"What do you want to do about it?"

"Nothing. Nothing. I never saw him. Just forget it." She reached for the office door handle.

"But he threatened you and your children. You

heard his voice, right?"

She shook her head again, "Doesn't matter."

"Yes, it does matter. Sit down for just a minute."

She hesitated, and I started talking fast. She took a step away from the door. I told her that hearing his voice was as good as seeing his face. Recognizing someone's voice could become evidence. I felt desperate to get something. She stood silent for a few minutes looking at the floor. I stood there holding my breath.

"You have a pretty good idea whose voice it was, don't you?"

No, I don't. I don't."

The terrified look came over her again, but her eyes looked a little different. Then she whirled around and lurched toward the closed door again. The interview was over. Marty wanted to escape from me and the FBI.

By this time, she was crying full bore.

"Let me outta here."

I stepped forward and grabbed her arm.

"If you name the guy, he'll be arrested and charged. We'll make sure he's locked up so the asshole can't hurt you."

She looked up at me through her tears. "What about my children?"

"We'll protect them too, I promise."

"That won't work."

"Yes, we can. Listen. Listen to me."

I firmly pulled her back to the chair, and started in with made-up promises. The protection by the FBI. Security for her and the children. The defendant in custody, locked up before trial. I was so riled up she could see I wouldn't give up. I kept repeating myself.

Finally, finally, she gave me his name. Ron, a tribal member she knew. She was terrified of him. Panicked at the idea of going through a trial. Wishing she had never reported the rape. Facing him out on the reservation was dangerous for her and the children.

I made more assurances. Just then the FBI agent knocked on the door. Marty jumped. I told the agent to wait out in the lobby. I then wrote out a short statement from her that had a lot of gaps.

I told Marty that Ron would be arrested, and would probably plead guilty. Then she wouldn't have to testify. I downplayed the possibility of a trial.

"He will be sentenced to prison. For a very long time."

I handed her a pen and stood over her while she signed the statement. I picked it up and slipped it in my file out of sight.

Marty just sat there, then looked up and said, "But what if I'm not sure?"

"Aren't you?"

"I don't know now. I was drunk and passed out. I only heard his voice."

"Well, you recognized it, right? Right?"

"Well, I…I got to pick up my kids." She dropped her head.

I called the FBI agent back in, and he drove Marty home to the reservation. Charlie and I met later and planned our strategy for charging the defendant and protecting Marty and her family. When I presented the case to the U.S. Attorney for approval to prosecute, James was the one with reservations.

James knew that the victim immediately after the rape claimed she did not see the attacker or have any idea who he was. She had told this to the BIA agent, the hospital attendants and the FBI officer. Her recorded statements were in the investigative records that eventually would be available to the defense. James also knew that the victim was pressed by me to reveal that she thought she knew who the guy was.

"*Thought* she knew who the guy was?" James raised his bushy eyebrows. "And you think that's enough?"

"She is petrified of him. That he'll harm her and her children if she tells."

James said it was unlikely that a jury would convict on the questionable facts. The other AUSA's agreed. We went round and round, arguing the pros and cons. This was before DNA evidence was admissible for identification from semen found on the victim.

James told me, "Write up a declination form and move on. Case closed."

I tried in vain to persuade AUSA Jay, the hard ass prosecutor who handled tough criminal cases, to support my determined plan to prosecute the rape case. I talked to Karl, and he told me it was a definite loser. He was adamant, brusque and critical as we argued about it. But I didn't want to give up. Between the credibility problems, especially the defense lawyer's opportunity to cross examine the victim's contrary statements to show her as an unreliable or lying, successful prosecution wasn't in the cards.

All the experienced guys told me it was hopeless.

I brought up the possible option of charging the defendant, and later dismissing the case before trial if things went awry. That is, if he didn't plead guilty. Historically, the AUSAs avoided that scenario because it cut into our office's credibility. Plus, it would waste resources and not look good in reports to the DOJ. Not to mention the stinging criticism if the press got ahold of it. I agonized over what to do. I feared being fired if I kept up what they viewed as my troublesome stubbornness.

I kept working on the case. Karl was outspoken, calling my approach stupid and foolhardy. Everyone thought it was a risky blunder. But by then I was set in my plan—committed. I was blinded by my own power and couldn't give it up. By the time of that tipping point, James could have absolutely forbidden me to go on. But he didn't.

I realized later maybe he wanted me to fail so he could fire me. That, or he had some secret insight that I could pull it off.

I tenaciously moved my foolhardy prosecution forward. In the process of charging the defendant with rape under the Major Crimes Act, the FBI agents were discreet and resourceful. Maybe they inwardly cheered me going ahead, I couldn't tell. The agents managed protection for the victim and her children. The judge denied bail because of potential threats to the family by the defendant and his relatives on the reservation.

The defendant did not plead guilty. His lawyer demanded a jury trial.

"No possible way will I plead my client out." He

had seen the investigative reports containing all the contradictions.

I put my nose into the law books and sweated it out as I prepared for trial. No help or support from my colleagues since they thought I was headed for disaster. Tension permeated the office. The staff ignored me. I was on my own.

In the midst of my trial prep, the victim arrived unannounced in my office. Marty begged me to drop the case. Her fear surrounded her like the smelly, rumpled clothes she wore, as if she'd been sleeping on the streets.

Upset and crying, she yelled back as she left, "I won't come to court."

Marty disappeared for weeks while I tried to contact her. Before she dropped out of sight, she parked her children with her sister. Even the FBI couldn't find her. I panicked that I would have to dismiss the case. I got more criticism from my colleagues.

"Bad case from the beginning," James said.

"You need to drop this case now. We'll all look bad," added Karl.

"Just wait a little longer, we have time, she'll turn up," I argued.

"You are being unreasonable. Irresponsible. This job isn't for bleeding hearts."

"I…I'll just wait a few more days. Give the FBI a few more days to work on it. Please. I'll keep you posted."

James and Karl stomped out of my office. Karl frowned like he wished I would disappear. I think everyone down the hall heard us arguing. Now I knew my job might be in jeopardy.

I immediately called Charlie to get more help from the FBI. He and I talked daily as the trial date loomed. A week before trial, the agents got lucky and found Marty living on the streets not far from our federal courthouse in downtown Spokane. The FBI found space in a shelter for her and the children.

I went to see her at the shelter and pleaded with her to stay in touch. That she would be safe. That her testimony would be brief. I phoned her every day until the trial began. She began to sound less hesitant. I convinced myself she understood my instructions.

I kept James minimally informed although he had no enthusiasm for what I was doing. If this case had the availability of DNA evidence as it does now, the DNA findings would have elicited a guilty plea—open and shut. But not in the 1970s.

The trial began. James did not sit next to me on this one. The court-appointed defense attorney contended in his opening statement that the witness was drunk and passed out in a pitch-black room. He emphasized that the claimed voice recognition simply wasn't credible—a guess, a case of mistaken identity. That the witness (he never called her the victim) had not identified the defendant in her statements immediately after the alleged rape. That she came up with his name only later based on "speculation without any hard evidence." That the medical exam showed only a probability of an assault, not who did it. At the first-day trial break, the defense attorney kept at me to drop the weak case, even suggesting that his client might be persuaded to plead to misdemeanor assault. I said no.

When the FBI agent escorted the victim into the courtroom to testify, Marty looked small and scared. But at least she was there. As she took the oath with her right hand raised, she seemed to get taller. Her chin was set. No tears. She never glanced in the defendant's direction. When asked to identify him for the jury, her eyes focused on the back wall of courtroom behind the defense table, while her finger pointed to him.

On the witness stand, Marty's faint words firmed up. On cross examination, she remained believable as if an inner force held her together. When she testified that she had been afraid at first to identify her assailant, her fear showed. As well as her sincerity.

The entire effect was remarkable, especially considering Marty's demeanor when I met with her in troubled times before trial. My shoulders loosened as she left the witness stand after cross examination. But still, I was scared stiff of losing the case. The defense made a persuasive motion to dismiss on the basis of insufficient evidence, but the judge ruled against it.

"I believe that the jury should decide," he said, after reviewing the evidence.

Two full days of jury deliberations passed while I remained restless with twisted anxiety. Although time stood still, I worked in my office on other cases with the door closed. I didn't stray far from my phone. The guys in the office were beside themselves. I could hear them pacing, talking in low tones. My thoughts were jumbled, with echoes of, "I am not fit for this job."

When the call came that the jury had a verdict, I dreaded going upstairs to the courtroom. As the jurors filed in, they didn't look at me. A bad sign.

"Guilty."

I jumped at the words. I felt faint. I couldn't open my eyes or look up. My legs wobbled when I left the courtroom. I could hear whispering as the guilty defendant was led away back to lockup. At least there was no wailing.

I was never able to talk with Marty that day when she testified in court. The FBI agent told me Marty took her kids and left the area because of confrontations on the reservation with the defendant's many relatives A steep price for testifying.

The defendant remained in federal custody pending sentencing, which hit him with maximum prison time. I closed my file on the trial phase of the case which was appealed. The Ninth Circuit Court of Appeals later affirmed the jury's verdict.

Although I felt satisfaction with the conviction, my handling of the case had caused a rift between me and the other AUSAs. They thought me reckless, risking the prosecution on thin evidence and an unreliable witness. Like I had too much sympathy for the victim and blind passion for the rape case. Not enough common sense.

My colleagues didn't criticize me outwardly after the verdict. Their weak congratulations rang hollow with insincerity, mixed with probable relief at the conviction. They were clearly annoyed at my stubborn approach to the rape case with such slim evidence. Karl didn't speak to me. Dreary recriminations hung over me.

I didn't have time to dwell on the whole scenario, but gave myself credit for being tenacious and pulling it off. My attention focused on minor cases and administrative appeals, plugging along in a solitary way, trying not to rock the boat. In other moments, I was mad as hell at my colleagues for not having faith in me. It made me insecure and nervous about their evaluation of my professionalism, or perhaps the lack of it. That meant so much to me. I needed to try harder to make sure they thought well of me, approved of me and told me so.

At home, I drank more and felt cross at Michael. He was cranky in return, having problems of his own at work with unrealistic computer conversion deadlines and personnel issues.

"Michael, listen to me. I'm furious at James and all those guys for not having faith in me about the rape case. Not trusting my judgment. Not supporting me."

"Huh? Well, do something about it, talk to them, or get over it."

"They didn't give me any credit for getting a conviction. Instead, just ignored me. I feel like slugging them sometimes."

"Whoa, Diana. Calm down and cool off. You knew what you were getting into, so suck it up. Forget it. Let's take a walk and calm down."

"No, I don't want a goddamn walk. I just want understanding."

He stomped out and went walking by himself. Now I'd pissed him off, too. I can't win. I poured another glass of wine and leaned into the blur.

I never expected to see the rape victim Marty again, but later that year I was totally startled when she showed up at my office one morning. I didn't recognize her, with a short haircut, dressed in a bright striped sweater and fashion jeans. Thinner and cleaner, she looked at me with shy yet confident eyes. She stayed only a few minutes, but informed me that she moved to the Seattle area, and enrolled in community college. Her kids were in a good daycare. She was in eastern Washington visiting her extended family on the nearby reservation for the first time since the trial. None of the defendant's family had bothered her so far.

"I never woulda went through it except for you and that FBI dude," she said.

I felt a big lump in my throat. "You did a brave thing, helping yourself, and maybe other victims. He won't be out of prison for a long time."

"I know. The agent told me. But I'm still scared."

She smiled a little as she left the office. I smiled too, feeling washed over with a wave of gratitude. My refusal to give up on her case had given her more than a victim's despair. I called agent Charlie Emerson and filled him in on Marty.

In my closed office, I gazed out my office window to the Spokane River and the large encircling Riverfront Park below. Set in the city, it was where I took walks at times when I was troubled about cases or trying to figure out strategy.

I wondered if the rift between me and my colleagues would fade away. I never heard any postmortems about the case, discussions about the conviction or recounted war stories usually a topic after a case was concluded. It was like it never happened. I didn't dare think of any "told you so" moment—that wouldn't go over from me at all. I was on my own. That meant I needed to be tough. But not troublesome. I was still the new "girl lawyer," fully aware of the super scrutiny that surrounded me.

That rape case left me with battle scars of nervousness and insecurity. I smoked more and noticed deeper lines of crow's feet around my eyes. While I repressed my frustrations, my goal was to step up to a better attitude based on lessons learned. Dwelling on my colleagues' criticism and my own shortcomings didn't help me. But finding out that Marty, the rape victim, had improved her life after relocating, gave me hope and satisfaction.

Chapter 6

About Boys

I TRIED TO SMOOTH THINGS OVER WITH THE OTHER AUSAs by hanging around, sometimes joining them to gossip, analyze cases, make fun of certain judges and defense lawyers. I jumped at any opportunity to invite myself to get a quick bite of lunch or have coffee with the guys, presenting myself as a player, not as a novelty new hire. I ignored thoughts about the rape case gamble they probably held against me—I got a conviction, didn't I? My daily self-talk invested me as a member of this elite government lawyers' team. That was key. I wasn't good at taking criticism.

I would almost forget that I was the only woman hanging out with four or five men, but the office staff noticed for sure. I wasn't privy to their conversations and didn't attempt to read their thoughts, but it was obvious they kept track of me and the sporadic tension in the office.

One day our AUSA lawyers' group left the office early to go across the street to the guys' exclusive social club for a drink—another one of my self-invitations where I used the barge-in approach that made it awkward to say no. It was mid-afternoon during the holidays—a spontaneous idea to escape from the office. Our boss James was on vacation. The judges were away, which meant no trials or motions on the docket.

"How about I join you—my desk is pretty empty. I've been wanting to see the inside of the men's bar now that they let women in."

I laughed as if it was a joke.

"Uh, sure, Diana. Come on along," Jay replied.

Two of the AUSA's were members of the private club with the off-limits bar where women were not allowed. The long-standing club rules changed recently to permit women in the inner sanctum. As we walked in, I immediately thought of Rennie, a local female reporter and club member "spouse," who had worked successfully on a club committee to revise some of the exclusionary club rules. After the rules changed, our local women's group joked among themselves about renaming the Spokane Club's bar to "Rennie's." But that's another story.

That afternoon playing hooky at the club bar, the guys plopped down into the leather chairs and ordered drinks. I followed, ordering a bourbon and water, noticing the warm wood-paneling and elaborate Christmas decorations. As my eyes panned the room, I couldn't avoid the most prominent décor—large oil paintings of nude women reclining in suggestive poses viewed from behind, with bodies turned in coquettish profiles against backgrounds of shadowy red colors. Artistically done, no doubt expensive. I tried not to stare.

Surrounded by the paintings, I turned my gaze back to my colleagues, their conversation and jokes. I put on a jovial attitude. The paintings faded from my awareness. Another round of drinks. We all talked fast and laughed louder than usual, in the competitive way that lawyers do. Our noise didn't matter in the quiet mid-afternoon. I relaxed as the alcohol dissolved my uneasiness. Two of the guys played a dice game for payment for the drinks. One suggested we play poker.

The bartender pulled out a deck of cards and poker chips, then set up the game at our table. Women were still shut out of the bar's adjoining card room where the men usually played cards. We sucked down more drinks. The afternoon warmed, while I felt all mellowed out as one of them. Just hanging out with my lawyer buddies.

I hadn't played much poker, but enough to know which hand beats another and a little more. During poker games with law school classmates, I learned about bluffing, which of course, was useful in lawyering as well. At the table, I played along and practiced my bluffing. The game was in full swing when a local business lawyer who knew the guys sauntered in. They introduced me. He joined our rowdy game.

By then I was feeling no pain. Playing the cards flowed into a smooth routine of risk and reward. Especially when great cards showed up in my hand. My stacks of red, white and blue chips piled up. We outshouted each other as we played cards, told jokes and drank. I felt connected—in the game, the club, the winner's circle. My brain crowded out any random warning thoughts.

We had to stop our poker game when other members drifted into the bar later in the afternoon. Our behavior was clearly out of sync with expected club demeanor. No one kicked us out of the bar, but the bartender discreetly removed the cards and poker chips over our objections.

My pals paid up and I stuffed a handful of bills into my purse. Flying high—one of the guys—I laughed at the word "ringer" from one of them. Our afternoon antics were over. I decided to leave my car in the parking lot overnight, and called Michael to pick me up.

"Are you drunk? You sound wasted."

"No, I'm fine. Just a jovial poker game at the club with my friends."

"What friends?"

"The AUSAs and another guy. Guess what? I won money."

"Well, you're shit-faced."

"No."

Silence on the phone.

"Are you picking me up or not?"

More silence.

"The front door on Riverside," he finally said.

"Thanks, Michael," I said cheerily.

On the way home, I could feel his anger at my chattering about winnings in the poker game. I mumbled a couple of the dumb jokes.

"Well, Diana. Happy you got drunk with the guys?" He was pissed off.

"Well, sure."

"Yeah. You'll be embarrassed tomorrow."

"Oh, no."

"You are totally blasted. You can hardly stand up."

"I'm one of the guys."

The last thing I heard from Michael was "Don't puke in my car." I drifted off slumped against the passenger door.

When I awoke the next morning, he had already left for his office. I opened the door to the garage, no car. With a pounding headache, I got ready, then called a cab to get to work. Hoping my car was still in the parking lot from yesterday.

Even with my raw hangover the next day, I felt an inclusive afterglow from the impromptu afternoon—my initiation into the boys' club. Through my fogginess I could still laugh at the whole situation, despite a few rational second thoughts.

I racked up my survival as a plus. I didn't give in or pass out. I doubt the unrefined camaraderie gained me any increased acceptance with my male colleagues, but I thought so then. The wild poker game broke a barrier for me. My mask of deference cracked into bad behavior—loud, obnoxious and crude. For a couple of hours, I was just like them. We laughed and joked about the previous day, and I was kidded for my luck getting all the good cards. I felt smug with positive feelings echoing "if you can't beat them, join them." Or if you can't join them, beat them. Welcome approval both ways.

But no approval from the staff, who treated me with hostile stares and chilly words. I suppose they overheard comments about boorish behavior at the club the day before. I couldn't read their thoughts, but their whispered conversations looked bad. All I could see were furtive glances and downcast eyes. Maybe jealousy.

But I continued to push to blend in with the AUSAs and other male attorneys. I could feel their male energy and power which rubbed off on me as high drama, like survival instincts in a battle, a never-give-up challenging fight, with whatever weapons I had.

The social scene always loomed as an opportunity to be one of the guys, a way to membership in the lawyers' club. Even in my obsession, I knew going overboard could get out of control. Especially with alcohol. I pushed my nagging inner monologues out of my head. I wondered whether I'd ever be one of the guys. This going back and forth drove me crazy.

My compulsive need for approval had dragged me into the extra-legal world of gamesmanship, crude language and swagger. That was my superfluous take on a successful trial lawyer—a respected persona to envy. In this game of adopting the male model, it often meant blurting out my acquired lawyerlike locker-room language. A tricky drama of push and pull for a woman.

My exposure to the "f" word as acquired legalese had taken off in law school. I encountered the word used offhandedly by students, ninety per cent of whom were male. It was fuck this, fuck that, this fucker, fucking amazing, fucking stupid, fucking far out—on and on. The most ironic: fucking beautiful, as in "the witness statement is fucking beautiful," or the "fucking good job" one did on cross examination in trial practice class.

These speech patterns spread to all law students. I began to use the word routinely as a natural part of my vocabulary. Kind of like you do after hanging out with someone with a southern drawl, you start saying y'all this and y'all that. At gatherings of law students and lawyers, the frequency of the word overshadowed the big words learned from the law books. While our legal vocabularies increased, so did our reliance on the four-letter word. It was just another way I imitated the boys—a necessary compromise although it didn't seem so at the time.

My personal background in Catholic schools and a conservative family never exposed me to crude language. My parents never spoke that four-letter word. The word was common in movies and books, but I didn't look the part to say it, as a mature woman, mother and grandmother. The staff women in the USA's office probably cringed when they heard me. That didn't worry me. I was on my one-way street to success and belonging.

When I talked with my female lawyer friends, a different "f" word erupted. We identified with the word most men never used—*feminism*. We figured our "f" word checked in as the most dangerous and despised word in our conservative town—our running joke. We feminist lawyers and businesswomen tried to blend into and adopt the male model as professionals, so we didn't broadcast our own "f" word. We were living out our feminism in a male-dominated world, yearning for our own success.

Our toughness as feminists was perceived often

as bitchiness. On the other hand, when we displayed our soft undersides for self-selected issues, we were misunderstood as vulnerable and weak—a catch-22. Despite these dilemmas, I hung on to my inner warrior energy as strength; my passion for the underdog and unpopular issues as courage. Things to fight for.

Chapter 7

Pussy Prosecutor

FBI SPECIAL AGENT FRANK SCHNEIDER DROPPED by my office carrying a fat file under his arm. That was after he found out that Karl, my white-collar crime colleague, was tied up in a lengthy criminal trial. The fat file contained a bank embezzlement case. These usually fell under concurrent federal and state jurisdiction, federal because of the bank's FDIC insurance regulations. Both jurisdictions worked together, but the feds preferred to prosecute these high-profile crimes. Karl was their man in the USA's office. Now the file was on my desk.

The FBI's investigation of the bank embezzlement had taken months. The target was a clever teller who had skimmed off small sums of money on a regular basis over a two-year period. When discovered by bank authorities, they immediately dismissed her. The bank audit revealed over $10,000 in missing funds. She had outwitted the bank's security procedures. Bank officials hungered for retaliation with prosecution, conviction and a long prison sentence.

The teller, Jill Burke, was married with three

small children A longtime trusted employee, Jill had worked at the bank off and on between pregnancies since graduation from high school. Spokane County Family Court files accompanied the federal investigative reports.

These Family Court records described multiple domestic violence complaints, none ever prosecuted. Affidavits alleged that Jill's husband often absconded with her paychecks, leaving her and the children insufficient money for food and other necessities. The pattern of abuse and abandonment was graphic. A restraining order prohibited the husband from living in the home pending a petition for divorce. No divorce decree had been entered, and no criminal charges ever lodged.

After Agent Schneider left, I pored over the voluminous files and court records. I was struck with the woman's cleverness in the bank thefts, as well as the tragic soap opera script of her family life. I didn't call the agent back. I dragged my feet preparing a criminal complaint. I wanted to talk to the suspect.

I told the agent what I needed. He balked but agreed. Frank Schneider, a straight-laced agent with military posture, all business with no hint of sensitivity, set up the meeting. The meeting would take place only after recitation of the suspect's constitutional rights including the opportunity to consult with a legal services lawyer. The FBI office handled all the necessary details for the interview, acknowledgement of her rights and signing of necessary waivers. Jill Burke, desperate with nothing to lose, agreed to the last-ditch meeting with me.

On a cold wintry morning, Agent Schneider, bundled up in a down jacket and black knit hat over his thinning blond hair, brought Jill to my office. Stepping into the doorway as if walking the plank, a slight woman with no hat, stringy brown hair and a bad complexion appeared. Her beautiful face had gone to seed early. Chapped hands pulled her windbreaker tight over a thin shirt and wrinkled pants. Her wary eyes showed only chilly uncertainty.

"Jill, I'm Diana Keatts, the prosecutor who will be handling your case." I pasted a friendly expression on my face, and explained my role in the process. She responded to my questions with single words and short phrases.

"How old are you, Jill?"

"23."

"Tell me about your family."

"Three kids."

"How long did you work at the bank?"

"Five years."

"Do you understand what you're charged with?"

"Yes."

On and on it went, my persistent questions and her reluctant answers. After drinking some black coffee, she was still defensive, though her closed fists loosened slightly. I confronted her about the embezzlement of bank funds, and she admitted everything. She told me about her random theft of small amounts and how she covered it up. I explained the consequences of a conviction of embezzlement. She dropped her head like a convicted felon with no way out.

When I asked about her husband, revealing that I had the Family Court files, her eyes flashed. All of a sudden, she had words to describe her marital problems, worries about her children, and her disastrous finances. Jill's fear tumbled out as she choked on her words. Only when she told me about her children did her face soften.

"I needed the money for my kids. Ralph kept taking my paycheck. I could only yell at him. He pushed me around and punched me if I argued. My mother couldn't really help. She babysat the kids when I worked."

I kept asking questions, hearing the ugly details of her domestic life. Why she opened up to me, I don't know. More than once she muttered, "If Ralph finds out, he'll kill me." I could feel her visceral fear. She couldn't face repercussions if he found out she came to my office. She blinked back tears of genuine frustration. Agent Schneider looked down as he leaned against my closed office door.

Jill repeated she'd taken only small sums of bank cash. She didn't know how much in all. Couldn't say how long it had been going on. She lived day-by-day, hanging on by the few threads of her job. Her mother wanted Jill to divorce her husband, but there was no money to finalize the divorce. Despite the restraining order, the husband returned home periodically with apologies, money and false promises. The court files documented Jill's sad dilemma.

The agent looked up at me about then. Time's up. He escorted Jill out. I sat at my desk and stared out my window at the somber gray sky.

I sat there, my conflicted thoughts stalling me

from drafting a criminal complaint. All the facts and law supported felony charges against Jill. With no legal defense, she would have to plead guilty. Her attorney would request leniency at sentencing, based on her circumstances.

The bank officials urged the agent to get the complaint filed and on track. Schneider came by for status reports. I put him off, and avoided my indecision by working on other cases. Thoughts of Jill's hellish family plight churned in the background.

At one point, I researched the uncommon process of "deferred prosecution." The procedure required filing of the complaint, a plea of guilty, and agreement to specific conditions in exchange for a deferral. If the conditions were met, the case would be dismissed. If not, the defendant faced conviction and sentencing.

When I raised this possibility with Frank Schneider, he resisted. "Not acceptable to the bank," and obviously not to him. I insisted on discussions with bank officials about conditions of restitution—leverage for the bank's agreement. We met with bank officials. No deal. I puzzled about why the bank had so much say-so. I talked with James Wilson, my boss, about the complicated situation. He was not enthused about deferred prosecution.

"Diana, the defendant can ask for leniency at sentencing after a plea of guilty. We've got her cold. Go ahead and prosecute," said James. Then Karl got into the act.

"It's a no-brainer," he said. "File it, get it over with."

"But it's complicated. So many personal issues. Look

at the domestic violence file, and notes of my interview with Jill. All the bad stuff her husband does to her. Basically, holding her hostage along with the kids."

I tried to personalize Jill. I could see that didn't change Karl's mind, as he left the room.

A few days later, my boss James met with agent Frank Schneider and me because I hadn't given in about my deferral idea, even though they were ticked off.

"The complaint needs to be filed. It's an easy case."

Having made all my points about Jill's situation, the addition of a clause in the deferral about restitution, and all the rest, I felt frustrated, disillusioned, and surprisingly scared. I thought about giving in. In the end, I just sat there silent, not agreeing to file a criminal complaint against Jill.

Suddenly, James blurted out, "Alright, that's it. If you're going to be such a pussy prosecutor, go ahead. Do the damned deferral." Agent Schneider sat there stoically.

I was shocked. I jumped up, grabbed my file and left James' office, slamming my office door behind me. His stinging insult to me was the ultimate putdown of an ineffective fraidy-cat female who couldn't be a tough hard ass prosecutor.

I worked off some anger in a frenzy preparing the paperwork for deferred prosecution. As I cooled down a little, I thought, I'm in hot water when I take a risky case to trial. Then I'm a pussy prosecutor when I defer prosecution in a clear-cut case. Either way I'm blindsided. Shit, I can't win. I'm not cut out for this.

But then I thought of Jill's situation and kept writing.

I had the agent contact the bank and inform them of the deferral plan. Another problem, since the bank official pushed back by calling my boss to complain, according to the agent. James never mentioned the bank's call to me. I knew the stakes were high, but I kept going. I met with the court-appointed attorney and he conferred with Jill, who agreed to the conditions. The papers were filed in court. The judge approved the deferred prosecution. At the hearing, he lectured Jill, who shook uncontrollably while her tears flowed.

Later that year I was notified that the embezzled funds had been repaid in full. The agent told me the payor was not identified. The case was dismissed and never crossed my desk again.

I found out later from Frank Schneider that Jill divorced her husband. She found a job in a community center. The FBI agents always knew stuff about case histories and ending chapters about former defendants, and they'd share the latest gossip with the prosecutors. I felt good that the deferred prosecution had worked out for the bank teller. I wasn't privy to their conversations, but I imagined that James and Karl may have held this one against me—another black mark for my performance review.

As time went on, I came to realize that my ability to decline to prosecute, or prosecute with conditions, was my greatest power as an Assistant United States Attorney. Other disagreements arose over whether to prosecute, but never again did I get in a fight like the first few. My next declination involved two mentally-handicapped men who pilfered U.S. Treasury checks from a neighbor's mailbox and cashed them. Because of the nature of their disabilities and technical issues with the conduct of their arrests, I declined to prosecute. No comment from James on my decision that time.

The federal agents sometimes balked if I told them I would not prosecute a case they presented. Agents invested time and effort to hunt down evidence. They interviewed witnesses, gathered and analyzed physical clues. Sometimes had actual confessions. Committed to their cases, they expected prosecution. An agent would sometimes pass the file to a different prosecutor for a second opinion if he didn't like mine. But as I gained credibility with courtroom convictions and creative plea bargains, the agents listened to my case evaluations with more understanding. Yet I could not forget being called pussy prosecutor, and Michael knew it.

"Diana, you just have to move on. Law enforcement has their role and you have yours. Get over the pussy prosecutor thing," he said one night when I was feeling down.

"Well, yeah, but I suspect the agents criticize my declinations in private. After all, their job forces them to produce the goods on the suspects. Get them off the streets. And don't forget, they obsess about their conviction status reports to D.C."

"That's their problem."

"My job means analysis and judgment before a grand jury session. Before an indictment or criminal complaint is drawn up. I have to decide whether the evidence, you know, and whatever factors outside the agent's report, will bring a conviction."

"Uh, huh."

"It's a different burden of proof. I have to prove the case beyond a reasonable doubt."

"Diana, just keep doing what you're doing. That's all you can do—use your best judgment and let the chips fall wherever. By now you've had enough experience. They should respect your decision-making."

Michael's practical advice always calmed me down.

My written declination reports piled up on James' desk, as he required me to make a copy of each report for his in-basket. After the bank embezzlement case, he sometimes commented on the declinations. But not by calling me names. By the time I completed my years in federal practice, my number of declinations far exceeded the number of cases I prosecuted.

I wondered, was I the "decline-to-prosecute" prosecutor?

I saw an ironic twist to the tough prosecutor image I cultivated. My split persona felt schizophrenic. Sort of playing multiple roles in a never-ending play while wearing the same costume. Was I being dishonest, too tenderhearted, or just savvy?

As I explained to Michael, "I internalize frustration about disagreements with my colleagues, but suffer more when I stifle my opinions. I'm either not heard or super scrutinized. The super scrutiny is worse."

Chapter 8

Courtroom Fashionistas

I KNOW THAT APPEARANCES ARE IMPORTANT, OF course. I admit thumbing through popular "Dress for Success" books in the 1970s. Even serious lawyer magazines featured tips about what to wear for optimal courtroom effects. Advice to women lawyers advised them about power suits, sincerity colors and take-charge images. But this extraneous stuff didn't really grab my interest.

After all, attention to lawyer's clothes didn't jive with her basic professional responsibilities—to represent a client, give advice, and above all, be competent. Apparel had no logical connection to legal precedent or jurisdiction. No law school class told students how to dress.

In those days, I observed that women didn't wear pantsuits in the business and professional world, because pantsuits were practically unheard of. Women wore dresses or skirt suits if they worked "outside the home."

When I began work as a lawyer, the what-to-wear issue didn't pose a concern. Except I had to shop for courtroom outfits like suits with jackets, skirts, long-sleeved blouses, and conservative high heeled black pumps because I didn't have any. I splurged on a three-piece herringbone tweed pantsuit with a button-up vest—a lawyerlike look. Quite a change from my usual law school get-up of jeans and baggy sweaters.

During my first week as prosecutor, I enjoyed sporting new clothes. But my brief attention to clothes faded as I became overwhelmed with the substantive challenges, especially since I didn't feel like a real lawyer yet. The few women at professional meetings and law-related social events showed up in business suits with skirts, jackets and high-necked blouses like me.

However, I had no particular reluctance about wearing my new pantsuit in the office or to arraignments or minor criminal matters before the U.S. Magistrate in his small courtroom. His role as a lower level judicial officer than the District Court Judge meant that proceedings were more informal, and often did not involve all the accoutrements of the high-ceilinged formal courtroom on the Ninth Floor where most jury trials were held.

The Magistrate was a former law professor who taught torts and evidence. When he was first appointed as Magistrate shortly after I became an AUSA, I inquired as to how I should address him in view of his elevated status. "Judge" or "Your Honor" or "Magistrate," I wasn't sure.

"Your Majesty would be fine," he said with a twinkle in his eye. A gentleman with a sense of humor. We laughed together and got on with the case issue at hand. He never noticed or commented on my courtroom attire, occasionally a pantsuit.

Not long after, I appeared before the District Court Judge in the big courtroom upstairs to argue a routine discovery motion in a civil case, again decked out in my tweed pantsuit. Two opposing male lawyers joked with each other, ignoring me before the hearing. No jury was present. After oral arguments and rulings by the judge, I picked up my files, slung my purse over my shoulder and left the courtroom. Down the hallway, the judge's clerk caught up with me. Looking hesitant, he motioned me away from the other lawyers.

"Diana, uh, I have to tell you, uh, well, the judge asked me to speak with you…."

"Jesse?"

He gulped, "Uh, well, the judge wanted me to let you know that wearing pants in the courtroom, well, he would like you to, uh, consider…."

"What?"

"Uh, he thinks it's inappropriate. A suggestion. Sorry." He looked away.

"You're kidding…."

I felt a hot flash across my chest.

"No, no. Just an informal suggestion. He thought you'd understand."

"Is that an order?"

"Well…uh, no. But he made me come out and mention it. God, I'm so sorry, Diana."

"Oh, really."

"The judge said it's not a mandate," he added.

"Oh?" Words in my head tried to escape, but I was speechless.

We both stood there in silence.

The embarrassment showed in his flushed cheeks under Jesse's dark five-o'clock shadow. He was one of my favorite court clerks, bright and always helpful. His eyes apologized. But I got the message all right.

I managed to walk away as if nothing had happened. Put on my lawyer's mask and clicked by in my high heels past opposing counsel who were laughing over something between themselves. My skin burned with anger as I covered up my distress and stalked down the hallway. I left the office early that day, driving like a maniac for the safety of my own driveway.

Obsessing over the incident, I relived how cautious I'd been to wear the "right" outfits to court. I avoided bright colors, flashy jewelry, low-necked blouses. Instead my choices were knee-length skirts, minimal jewelry, conservative pumps. My hair trimmed short and controlled. Why was I busy de-emphasizing my feminine traits, yet required to wear a skirt? What was I doing, wearing the wrong uniform to a game that obviously mattered? Confused and furious, things got blurry. Was I overthinking this clothes thing? Or perhaps not enough?

My goal was to be taken seriously. After the comment relayed by Jesse, I didn't dare wear pants or slacks to the big courtroom for even a minor matter, and went back to skirts. If the judge worried about my attire, would that affect his ruling? I developed a paranoid edge worrying about my appearance.

I couldn't help thinking about other jurisdictions with different rules. As a historical tradition in Great Britain, all barristers don wigs and identical robes. In standard attire and head gear, all British lawyers are distinguishable from non-lawyers but not from each other. When hair and street clothing are covered at counsel table, the lawyer's gender doesn't pop out. Seems like a good thing.

For me and my women lawyer pals, the what-to-wear debate rolled on in the background, at odd times after a few glasses of wine. A thorny issue with no clear answers.

My law school buddy Josie Evans and I tried to sort this out at Parno's, our go-to place with a quiet bar where we sometimes landed at the end of the day. Josie, a freckled redhead with a strong low voice, had a small private practice, fighting it out on her own with great spunk in Spokane's conservative venue. I blurted out the pantsuit incident to her, as it still burned me.

"I'll admit I can be a dress-for-success chameleon, but I'm not good at it. I tend to dress sort of like the guys and minimize my femininity," I said.

"This is so ridiculous. Fucking ridiculous," she said.

"It seems like the right time to wear pants to court. I see working women wearing them all over now. Store ads feature pantsuits," I said.

"I know, I know. But this is intimidation. There's no reason to forbid pants in the courtroom."

"Have you worn them to state court?" I asked. With her family law and criminal defense law practice, she was in court a lot.

"Yes. Maybe a few stares, but no comments. Some guys are out of step, for sure."

Josie put up with a lot of irritating stuff as a criminal defense attorney and sole practitioner. She told me about one time she decided to use clothing as an attention-getter in state court when she got fed up with a male judge's customary roll-call greeting to lawyers on Motions Day. That greeting had finally been too annoying for Josie. She laughed as she began her story.

"He barked out every single Friday, 'Good morning, *gentlemen*.' No one ever seemed to notice that I was offended, and simply responded 'Good morning, Your Honor' in unison."

Not Josie.

She decided to show up one morning at the courthouse motions roll call in the front row wearing a tight red low-cut sweater under her open suit jacket—a provocative appearance. She boldly hid her fear, putting herself in a dicey situation of possible humiliation, maybe jeopardizing her client's case.

Josie could see the judge looking down at her open jacket showing bare ample cleavage.

"He totally forgot to say good morning that day."

After Josie's case was called, she buttoned up her jacket. Later she endured a couple of low catcall whistles in the hallway. Men liked Josie. She had more guts than I. She said the judge changed his greeting to "good morning" or "good morning, counsel" after that. Issue noted. Maybe.

Josie and I laughed, ordered another glass of wine. We chatted about the media's power to control the message with its packaging, making that the message. The successful marketers' messages make masterful propaganda. But lawyers as amateur marketers have a tough time figuring this out. Mixed messages can backfire.

"This crap pisses me off." I shook my head.

"Go in and talk to the judge about it. No way can he rule against you for that. Or even comment on your choice of courtroom clothes."

"I don't dare."

"Talk to the guys in your office.

"I can't do that either."

"This is so fucking ridiculous. I can't believe we're even talking about it. So...I guess, get over it, move on. Forget it, you look good in skirts, Diana."

I kicked her with my pointy-toe high heels.

We sipped wine, smoked a few more cigarettes and gossiped about our friends. About a few guys we hated and those we liked. Her favorite comment about ones she liked, "I wouldn't kick *him* out of bed."

I'd agree or not, and we'd relax. Josie was my most supportive friend, on the same wave length with offbeat humor and bad-mouthing the obstacles. We both knew that quality work and success for clients mattered most.

As time went on, I ignored the futility of my wardrobe concerns. I loosened up my rigid adherence to the senseless dress code. Wearing pant outfits and comfortable shoes became a frequent choice for "in-office" days as well as depositions. But courtroom jury trials still called for suits with skirts, always skirts. Only time would change this.

When the first woman was finally appointed state Spokane County Superior Court Judge by the

Washington governor, we all celebrated. We cheered at our women's support group meeting and were reminded of the courtroom fashionista fetishes.

Josie and I had to talk out all the possible effects of the new appointment. For one thing, we recognized that both male and female judges wore the same garb—black robes—no courtroom attire issue there. We anticipated that the presence of women as judges would add credible equity to the courtroom. Perhaps even diminish unwanted scrutiny of a woman trial lawyer's appearance. At least we hoped so.

Chapter 9

Bank Robbery: Slam Dunk

MY FIRST BANK ROBBERY CASE—OPEN AND SHUT. The primary evidence: a smudged, wrinkled bank deposit slip with the defendant's name printed on it. On the back of the slip, he scrawled the words—GIVE ME THE MONEY.

The teller had identified the suspect. She was a young, nervous woman who ID'd the robber both from a photo spread and an in-person lineup. Obsessed FBI agents informed me that they were sure this same guy had committed multiple bank jobs in the area. The other robberies didn't have a bank deposit slip, but the modus operandi, a handwritten note and general description of the suspect matched.

The few words about a gun in his pocket were identical although he never displayed a firearm.

"Believe me. I got a gun and I'll use it!"

Fuzzy bank security photos and lack of evidence in previous robberies hampered investigations over a twelve-month period. Now ample evidence was sufficient to charge the suspect in this case.

The defendant claimed to be indigent. No federal

Public Defenders' Office existed at the time, so the court appointed a defense attorney from the list of those willing to represent defendants. After the arraignment, the one-way pretrial discovery dragged on, that is, the prosecution discloses the evidence to the defense attorney. Motions were heard and a trial date set.

In conversations with the defense attorney, I confidently encouraged a plea of guilty in view of the overwhelming evidence. Claude, a seasoned criminal defense attorney in private practice, would have none of that. He knew it all. I could feel his wily observation of me as a newbie prosecutor.

"No way," said Claude. "My client's check book was stolen. He wasn't anywhere near the bank on the day of the robbery. In another state, as a matter of fact."

Claude's confidence amazed me in light of what I had.

He wouldn't reveal the defendant's whereabouts on the robbery date, or much else. Just that he had defenses and I'd find out. We discussed plea bargain options. Delayed the trial for a few months. Not too worried, I expected the defendant to plead guilty.

Eventually, Claude produced names of a couple of defense witnesses from Montana. Our investigators tried numerous times to contact them without success. Nothing materialized except continued denials of guilt by Claude, and his assertions about the defendant's stolen checkbook. The trial date arrived, without concern from my prosecutor colleagues, It was a textbook case. Slam dunk, they said. I felt confident.

In the courtroom, the contrast between Claude and me was stark. He was the gray-haired, wiry, experienced "trial horse." I was still considered the new female prosecutor whose greenness showed. Claude had unexpected ways of catching me off guard.

He insisted with excessive polite gestures that I always precede him as we walked to and from the side of the judge's raised desk, or "bench" to confer while whispering with the judge during trial. These "sidebar" arguments usually involved admissibility of evidence, where one of us needed a ruling outside the jury's hearing before the witness blurted out potentially objectionable testimony. The jurors were alert and curious about what we were hotly discussing, straining to get a clue as to what was going on. Claude's overly deferential body language annoyed me. Especially when we were arguing over points of law, not choosing menu items as if we were on a date.

Perhaps I was overly sensitive, but this was guerilla warfare, and I knew what he was doing. Nothing to do but simply ignore such seemingly innocent tactics. After all, he was just "being polite" to me. I felt his overactive politeness to me as a female undercut my role as the tough prosecutor, but couldn't afford to show my temper or alienate the jury.

The prosecution case rolled along, with FBI agent Frank Schneider's testimony about the physical evidence. His deep voice projected clearly with professional answers. The jury took it all in. When bank teller Ellen testified, her high voice wavered as she described the robbery details. Her fearful eyes said it all. She avoided the defendant's gaze, until she pointed to him as the one who pushed the demand note at her. And threatened her. Her positive identification gave her confidence. Ellen's survival mode kicked in on cross examination and reinforced her direct testimony.

The trial flowed smoothly, until the defense took over. A grizzled woman named Mandy stepped up as the first defense witness. She strode up to the witness stand in an uneven gait with a take-no-prisoners attitude. With creased, sun-spotted skin, her age indistinct, she took the oath looking straight ahead. She ran a small goat farm in western Montana, and looked the part of a muscular farm woman, even with her tie-dyed shirt and denim skirt. Her unruly hair held back with a plastic head band, she coughed like a smoker before saying a word.

She slouched down into the witness chair, glanced at the jury and smiled. You hardly noticed her missing teeth. Her startling clear blue eyes shone against her tanned skin. Mandy adjusted her skirt, eager to tell her story.

"Yeah, I knew him for years. Not related, but sure, a friend. He stayed at my place, you betcha, mostly in the winter."

Folksy in her manner, her relaxed posture communicated believability. On to the main point, the day of the bank robbery in Spokane.

"Yeah, he visited my place that patticuler day, 'cause it was the day after my birthday."

"Anybody else there?"

"Yeah, Jimmy D came by. They went out riding."

Mandy colored her testimony with country slang, "You betcha," and "no durn doubt about that."

The tough cookie never wavered in my cross examination of her.

I could feel myself sweating.

Next up was a witness who lived near the Montana goat farm. Jimmy D, a youngish guy with worn jeans, rundown boots and a who-cares smile, looked at the defendant in a friendly way as he ambled up to the witness chair. After my continuing objections to both defense witnesses at sidebar which the judge overruled, Jimmy D testified that he and the defendant rode motorcycles in the hills near Mandy's place that day. Jimmy D's generic personal appeal spread over the courtroom—who wouldn't believe him? On cross examination, he stuck with his story, just a little stammer in his voice. Said he's "just doin' his duty," and no particular connection with the defendant, although he volunteered that he was a distant cousin of Mandy, the goat farmer. I was dying as the defense evidence came in before the jury.

The defendant did not take the stand. He didn't need to, after the alibi testimony.

In closing, the defendant's lawyer, Claude, rode hard up the mountain of the Montana alibi testimony. He also denigrated the use of the deposit slip as the robber's note to the teller.

"No one would be stupid enough to use his own checkbook slip as a note in a bank robbery. That would be giving your name and address to the bank," Claude pleaded to the jury. He paused for effect. He offered lots of what-ifs. His job was to raise doubts, reasonable doubts.

He carefully drew a scene which depended on the alibi witnesses whom he painted as sincere and truthful. He said they did not volunteer, but were subpoenaed, thus forced to come to court to testify.

"How could the defendant be in Montana and in Spokane, Washington, the same day?"

In closing, I carefully explained to the jury the mileage between the western Montana goat farm and the Spokane bank. Arguing that even if the witnesses' testimony was believable, that didn't necessarily mean the defendant wasn't in Spokane the same day. I emphasized the bank teller's ID of the defendant and the note to the teller. The teller had pushed aside the note when she got the cash together for the robber—maybe the robber didn't intend to leave the note.

This straightforward case was going south on me. The jury's attention to the smooth argument of the defense worried me. The facts were not all cut and dried as I expected. Now muddled by a goat farmer and a motorcyclist. But was that reasonable doubt?

The jury deliberated the rest of that day and into the next. In the prosecutor's office, we took that as a bad sign. Usually we expected a guilty verdict within a few hours—or after lunch, so the jury could have a free lunch before finishing their work. My colleagues' jokes gave comic relief to my concerns.

"Just wait till after lunch, Diana, that will tell the tale," my colleagues assured me. That didn't happen.

In the end the jury did convict the defendant. But it took almost three days. The "open-and-shut" case was not.

After the jury's verdict, the FBI agents wanted to bloody the two alibi witnesses with charges of perjury. But I never filed any perjury charges. That issue eventually lost momentum. As a matter of practice, prosecution of witnesses for perjury is rare.

The "deposit-slip" bank robbery case was over, and the string of similar bank robberies in eastern Washington and western Montana were never solved. The FBI agents proudly reported that these pattern robberies stopped after the defendant's arrest and imprisonment. They were sure they got their man. I agreed.

A pattern in law enforcement sometimes occurs when the officers investigate a crime where they know or have a well-grounded suspicion as to who committed it. If they can't gather admissible evidence in that crime, they try harder to obtain evidence in another crime by the same defendant, especially since property crimes are not one-time events. Overreaching is a temptation because of the agents' mission—to successfully fight crime. To get these bad actors off the street.

Officers' overreaching wasn't a factor in the bank robbery case. The deposit-slip evidence fell into their lap. But I gradually became aware of frustrations of law enforcement officers, even as they tried to comply precisely with constitutional constraints. This tension between getting the criminals off the streets versus making searches and arrests within constitutional limits challenged them. Casual conversations, jokes and relaxed bull sessions led me to this realization. The hidden obsessions of certain officers became apparent the longer I worked with them, although professionalism and ethical guidelines prevailed most of the time.

Chapter 10

Footfalls

AFTER I HAD SEVERAL PROSECUTION CASES UNDER my belt, I grew callous about the possibility of threats or dangers to me, as my newcomer apprehension faded. My focus was control, not weak vulnerability. Federal agents accompanied me when I left the office to visit a crime scene or participate in an investigation. Usual sidekicks were FBI guys, and occasionally agents from the Secret Service, Drug and Enforcement Administration or Alcohol Tobacco and Firearms. Thoughts of potential danger didn't register on my radar.

In addition to criminal cases, I cut my teeth on civil lawsuits against the government. Things like a slip-and-fall injury on a floor at the Small Business Administration office, a trespass case against the Forest Service for illegal entry on private land, a breach of contract action by a cleaning products supplier against the General Services Administration. Large and small, serious and trivial, the AUSAs became the face of big government in U.S. District Court. These cases compelled me to understand civil law and procedure inside and out. Even as I perceived them as a less juicy part of my trial work compared to the criminal cases, the plaintiffs in civil cases pushed them with personal passion.

A civil lawsuit against the U.S. Customs Service ended up on my desk on a bright day while I admired the colorful fall leaves in Riverfront Park below my eighth-floor window, daydreaming of taking the rest of the afternoon off for a long walk in the park. But I couldn't ignore the Customs' file marked "Urgent Action Required" brought in by a Customs Inspector.

The plaintiff, a local businessman, who owned and operated a specialty import shop, disputed the seizure of a large shipment of imported furniture and accessories in the course of a Customs inspection. Eventually he sued for damages, violation of regulations and return of the goods.

Andy, the Customs Inspector, helped me understand the Customs actions. A patient and straight-talking guy with a confident manner, he answered my questions with professionalism. Andy was about my age, with clipped graying sideburns and a seasoned look about him, who didn't hold my ignorance of Customs operations and procedures against me. I was still learning the ropes.

The long and complicated Customs regulations took many hours to review. Voluminous lists of disputed property filled the file. Preliminary administrative proceedings with complex procedures clouded the previous case history. I was to defend the Customs Service in the plaintiff's lawsuit. Time was of the essence for filing an Answer to the plaintiff's Complaint. Enough of my daydreams—no walk in the park for me.

In the course of pretrial discovery, I set up the plaintiff's deposition to obtain his sworn testimony. In our office conference room, the event turned out to be a challenging fiasco. The agitated plaintiff, a tall imposing man with black hair, a lined face and prominent nose, was accompanied by his experienced lawyer wearing an expensive suit and a swaggering tough guy expression. The angry plaintiff turned his venom on the government. That included me and Andy, the Customs inspector at my side.

As the deposition proceeded, the plaintiff's aggressive lawyer objected frequently to my questions, spouting off self-serving comments on the record. The court reporter typed without expression. She was a pro. The lawyer's tirades were obvious exhibitionist tactics to impress the client. The deposition atmosphere boiled over, simmered down, then heated up all over again. The main target of the plaintiff's chilling stares was Andy, who sat silent and immobile in his Customs uniform. I continued the questioning, as the "enemy's protector," a term mumbled loudly by the plaintiff to his lawyer at one point. I had to pull answers out of the red-faced defensive plaintiff while his Rambo-like lawyer railed on with objections, while the long tiring afternoon dragged on.

Depositions are permitted by court rules. Some depositions seem to last forever when rude outbursts by the lawyer and stone-walling by his client occur. When self-serving comments flare up on the record, the transcript of a deposition results in an argument for the case instead of the fact-finding it is designed for. In my later years, I would learn to cut off the out-of-control deposition and threaten to take the issue up in front of a judge for relief. But when I was a new lawyer, I didn't feel confident enough to walk out. As a government representative, I felt a heavy burden to allow fair representation, so I let the plaintiff and his lawyer rant.

By the time I finally left my office after the deposition from hell, the day had turned dark and drizzly.

I felt drained and battle-weary. I rushed out the glass doors of the U.S. Courthouse carrying my purse and briefcase, thinking pleasant thoughts of getting home to a glass of wine in front of the fireplace with Michael.

As the brisk air hit my face, I sensed someone nearby. In my peripheral vision, I noticed the dark silhouette of a man lingering in the shadows of the entry pillars. In those days, federal buildings had few security guards. The only ones protected by security were the judges, who used the underground parking garage below the courthouse.

I looked over at him, realizing the familiar look of the guy whose deposition I had just taken. Tall, dark hair, with a black leather jacket, a prominent nose. My adrenalin flashed. I took a quick breath. Picked up my brisk walk over the front pavilion, and onto the sidewalk toward my street-side parking lot.

My lot was three blocks away, and the late afternoon streets were quiet except for one commuter bus that roared by. After that, I heard steps behind me and glanced at him following me. Maybe he was simply walking to his own parked car. My heart started racing as my vulnerability washed over me. Part of me whispered—you're fine, just keep walking.

Afraid to look back again, my high heels tapped along without breaking into a run. I wonder now, what was I thinking—was I afraid to show my fear? My imagination went wild and pictured the worst, my heart beating like a jungle drum. Perspiration drizzled down inside my blouse, while the dank air made me shiver. My high heels acted like speed governors on my fearful feet.

At my parked car in the poorly-lit parking lot, I fumbled with keys, opened the car door, and frantically threw my purse and briefcase onto the passenger seat. I dropped myself into the car and clicked the lock. As I let my breath out and looked up, the familiar man with black hair and looks to kill stood next to my car window. I remembered my new pistol under the driver's seat, grabbed for it, then turned to him. He could see my gun well enough.

Planted there, he glared for a short second with harm in his hooded eyes, then turned away and disappeared into the dark night. I put my gun down on the center car caddy within easy reach. Shaking like a scared rabbit while turning the key, I slammed into reverse and peeled out of the lonely parking lot, never looking back.

Fighting to compose myself driving home, I struggled with lots of self-talk. Fortunately, Michael was working late so he didn't witness my disheveled state. I kept reliving the terror I felt, and my reaction to grab the gun. There would be no telling Michael about the encounter. That would mean big trouble because of the gun I bought without his knowledge. Feeling guilty about my concealment was much less than the fight we would have if he found out about my gun.

My plan was to tell the customs agent in the morning about the scare. The night filled me with disturbing dreams and wrestling with the sheets, so I got up early to escape to the office before dawn. By now Michael didn't question my errant coming and going with all my weird cases.

"See you, dinner at home tonight?" he mumbled in a sleepy hoarse whisper.

"I'll be here." I bent down and kissed his cheek as he drifted back to sleep.

Physically unhurt, I never knew whether the guy from the customs deposition meant to attack me. He never put a hand on me. But I had been thoroughly terrified, despite managing to grab my little pistol which had scared him off. I had to report the incident for my own safety the next day. Telling Andy in Customs what had happened, I felt reluctant to blow up the matter like an overly-imaginative scared female.

My tough prosecutor persona had taken time to cultivate, after all. Nevertheless, my confused psyche vacillated between bravado and genuine fright. Feminine vulnerability popped out at wrong times. These machinations drove me crazy.

One of my male colleagues was assigned to wrap up the Customs civil case, which settled before trial. I learned that the importer was later arrested and charged with criminal drug violations in another inspection because his imported goods contained a hidden cache of drugs. Did everyone except me knew of Customs' agents' underlying suspicions about the sleazy guy?

After my fearful encounter, I became nervous and overly-observant when leaving the federal building in the late dark afternoons or evenings, which was often. I changed my parking space to a closer, lighted garage.

That scary incident walking to my car was the only time I felt an actual personal threat while working as an AUSA. When I think of some of the dangerous criminal defendants I prosecuted, it is remarkable that no other threats or close calls arose. But the Customs' case had showed me that a litigant in a civil lawsuit could be just as emotional and dangerous as a criminal defendant.

The next week, a shocking death hit me like a sledge hammer.

Chapter 11

Requiem for Rennie

TRIPPING OVER HIGH HEELS WHILE RUNNING FROM a threatening bad actor was a small terror compared to the tragic news. Rennie, the rising young female reporter at the local newspaper, had killed herself.

Rennie was at our women's support group a few weeks ago, where we huddled at 6:00 a.m. twice a month to have coffee and prop each other up. Rennie seemed a bit off that Friday, but this unbelievable development? I couldn't take it in.

Rennie, outspoken feminist sister, our heroine, dead? Shot in the head in a bathroom at the local men's social club? This just couldn't be true. My mind raced in circles of the past with her.

I first met Rennie when I was in law school. Her beat was the City Desk at the paper, when she showed up at the law school to find out why we were camped out at the school's entrance overnight. Our renegade group of law students met after dark, which caused a fuss on campus grounds. Campus security came by to tell us we'd better keep quiet and orderly, adding, "No drinking or stuff like that." Which we later ignored.

Someone notified Rennie. She arrived on the

scene accompanied by a newspaper photographer. We explained that the law school's convoluted registration process made it difficult to get certain elective classes we needed for that semester. Online registration hadn't yet been developed. Since signup was on a first-come, stand-in-line process, we decided to be first for next morning's registration—a small group lined up with our registration packets all filled out, plus sleeping bags and food. Mostly a crazy stunt, not a demonstration. We weren't first-year students on a preset class schedule. By then, we were on our way to third-year law and thought we knew it all.

My law school buddy Jack had called earlier to let me know about the all-nighter. We'd been complaining about the problematic registration process for weeks to the school administration without success. I was quick to join in.

Michael didn't like it at all.

"This is totally crazy. You'll never last the night out there on the cement sidewalk."

"I'll be with Jack. And Josie. All our pals on the Law Review staff. Sleeping bags and food."

"Listen to me, this is crazy. You're off the deep end."

"Well, I'm close to home, so I'll just come back if I need to."

"Don't do this stupid thing, Diana," Michael's eyes flashed with anger.

Well, I did it. I stomped out the door with my bundle of stuff and walked to the law school a few blocks away. Guilt pangs about our power struggle and my defiance gnawed at me. I hated these fights with Michael.

Walking calmed me down. By the time I arrived at the law school, my friends were crowded up toward the front of the line. I joined them, my argument at home forgotten. We were over the top with excitement and purpose, my friends and I.

Our heroine reporter Rennie, aka "Brenda Starr, Reporter" from old newspaper comics, chronicled our law school stunt. She sat on the sidewalk with questions, writing in her slim reporter's notepad. The photographer fellow took a few shots of our group and left. Rennie stayed.

We told Rennie about the messed-up registration process and our resolve to overcome it. Maybe improve it for those who followed. Our talk revved up to bigger issues. Someone had wine. We passed the bottle around.

Rennie listened as the few women law students spun tales of hopes and dreams as well as their challenges—a handful of women busting into the male legal world. This struck a chord with Rennie, who fought her own daily roadblocks at the conservative newspaper in the straight-laced community where we lived. We ate popcorn, crackers, other junk food, and drank more wine.

Rennie left to get back to the paper for deadlines. Her next-day news story and photo of students lined up at the law school entrance touched us. She wove in personal vignettes of women law students in addition to accounts of the frenzied wannabe lawyers camped out to get their choice of classes. Rennie captured my fascination.

After law school graduation, our Action Women's

Exchange (AWE) group evolved as we entered the professional world as lawyers. Rennie became a regular at our Friday morning meetings. Her energy and dedication to women's equality issues inspired us. Our women's group grew as others joined: a few businesswomen, two realtors, an assistant bank manager aspiring to higher levels, a gynecologist, a CPA, a psychologist, a feminist writer. We exchanged business cards, referred clients, patronized each other's services. Sharing stories glued us together. The electric energy of the dynamic group propelled us out of the early dawn meetings with resolve and confidence—an "awesome" process.

Rennie's newspaper office building faced the intersection where the men-only-as-members social club stood. Women could join the club as spouses, but married women could not join as principals. We tried and were rejected. Rennie talked her husband into joining so she could agitate as a spouse member from inside the club for full-privilege membership for women. Changes in club membership rules hadn't been resolved yet.

Rennie had some success, because the club had decided that women could be admitted to the former men-only bar. A small victory. Shortly after the club's change in policy, I was allowed into the club bar, the scene of that drunken poker game fiasco with my colleagues. But Rennie wanted more—full membership rights equal to men.

The club thing sounds trivial, but it represented other discriminatory issues to us. The business and professional women who wanted to be full voting members of the club, to entertain their customers and clients on a par with the men, felt second-class as merely "spouse" members.

As a newspaper reporter, Rennie covered local news as well as special interest stories about rising women in regional businesses. Letters to the editor created interest in Rennie's well-written articles.

When I heard about Rennie's shocking death, I mourned the sad loss of her potential. I thought about stories of struggles to achieve her own goals and be accepted at the same level as male reporters. I remembered her articulate articles about working women's challenges. I could feel her vitality and ironic sense of humor. How could things have come to this? Shooting herself in the head?

Rennie must have had demons I knew nothing about. There was much I didn't know. Why did she choose to do it in the men's club bathroom—a virtual public place for the movers and shakers in town? I never found out whether there was a note. My puzzling guilt feelings made me feel I wasn't as innocent as I thought. I kept thinking, "Why, why?"

I cried my eyes out at her funeral. When her red-eyed husband stumbled up the aisle supported on each side by friends because he could barely stand up, I crumpled and couldn't hold anything in. At the service, Rennie's colleagues lauded her as a crackerjack reporter. A little late I thought, as I sat there with wet tissues and raging agitation.

Our women's support group gathered afterward

where we reminisced about Rennie. Definitely not a joyful celebration of life. We moved around hugging each other, filled with sadness and tears. We were wounded when our sister died. Determination, fear and anger barely kept us standing.

After Josie and I left the gathering, we stopped at Parno's. We sat there solemnly sipping glasses of wine. We could feel Rennie's presence. Not much left to say.

"I heard she had some drug and depression things going on," said Josie.

"I had no idea. She seemed focused, professional, funny. Such a crack reporter."

"Intense. Driven."

"We lost a fervent feminist." I raised my glass.

"Feminism can be deadly. Touched by fatality."

Josie, the solid rock of realism, balanced my impetuous idealism. My friend's dark thoughts and comments had the twist of down-to-earth pragmatism. Her unexpected comments exposing life in the trenches sometimes landed with a thud. Some people didn't get Josie. She was an anchor for me. A practical problem solver, my best friend Josie.

"Drink up, and I'll drop you off at your parking lot," she said.

"Sure." I felt a little slurred.

"Are you okay to drive?"

"Oh, yeah, fine."

As I got into my car that night after Rennie's funeral and conversations with Josie, I didn't realize how drunk I was. But of course, in my own take-charge way, I thought I could get home without any problems. That turned out to be wrong.

While driving home, I miscalculated the distance between my car and one parked along the one-way just before it merged into the two-lane. I heard the crunch of my rear-view mirror as I sped past the parked car, and then saw that my mirror was bent in.

Holy shit, did I just hit that parked car? I felt my adrenaline spike. but just kept driving. I couldn't think straight, so focused on the road to make it home. I parked in the street rather than trying to get into the garage. Michael was sitting in front of the fireplace reading the newspaper.

"Kinda late, aren't you? How was the funeral?"

"Depressing. I'm going to bed."

I stumbled into the bedroom, stripped off my clothes and fell asleep. Slept in the next morning with a massive hangover. Good thing it was a Saturday.

Michael was on the warpath when I finally appeared in the kitchen looking for some coffee.

"What the hell happened to your car?"

"What?"

"The rear-view mirror is smashed and bent. Was there an accident?"

"Huh? No, no, of course not."

"Well, what happened to your car?"

"Michael, I have no idea. Someone must have hit my parked car or something."

I was pretty good at lying. But I was scared and upset.

He and I stood there in the kitchen, me with a splitting headache and he with a lot of anger.

"Looked like you were pretty loaded last night."

"Well, there was a deal after the funeral with our friends, and then Josie and I stopped for a drink at Parno's. But I was only a little buzzed."

He didn't believe me. I poured myself more coffee, and went back to the bedroom to shower and get dressed. That wasn't the end of it, because at some point Michael had the car repaired and we got into another big argument. I didn't want to report the damage to our insurance agency. Michael took that as further proof that I hadn't told him the whole story.

He finally dropped it and things cooled down. I needed to take the incident as a warning signal that I'd better slow my pace, as I was on a one-way track to disaster with my drinking. I resolved to take more control. Which sounds easier than it was. Especially when I was always trying to fit in with the guys after work, at bar association meetings and elsewhere with alcohol as a lubricant.

I didn't take the car sideswipe crash as seriously as I should have. Instead, I blocked out concern about my shortcomings and forged ahead with my ambitions. I was a battle-ready warrior, fast on the draw, and survival was my mode. Never give in or give up. Keep up the pace as a hardball prosecutor. Move on.

Rennie's death brought sharper focus, rekindling my focus on the larger issues, rather than worry about my own faults. I dug into my work with renewed professional dedication. Do it for myself, for Rennie, and the women lawyers who follow me. I'd accomplished a lot already, and didn't want to screw it up.

Thinking back on the years of struggles through

college and law school, gut-wrenching conflicts about balancing family demands, and the heart-breaks of choices made, I'm not sure how my family saw it through. Somehow, Rennie's death triggered thoughts of the staggering realities of my recent past.

Along with memories of how it happened that a 30-something wife and mother ended up in college, law school, and as a federal prosecutor in the 1970s.

Chapter 12

Lawyer Wannabe

THE FIRST LAWYER I EVER SPOKE TO WAS MY UNCLE in his high-rise office in Seattle when I was 18 years old. My parents made me talk to him for a very specific purpose. To undo my hasty elopement and explain the annulment process, all in order to get me back in college "where I belonged."

That undoing didn't happen. My new husband and I fled to Berkeley, San Francisco area, and the North Beach scene. We both got forgettable jobs. Michael enrolled at UC/Berkeley. We had our marriage blessed in the Catholic church. Michael became a convert to Catholicism. We made friends. Time flew by. I became pregnant and we had a beautiful daughter.

After a couple of years, we returned to Washington state and were accepted back into the family fold. Having a new grandchild helped. We began again with whatever jobs we could get and Michael enrolled at the University of Washington.

Before I became one, I never really understood what lawyers did. They appeared as shadowy men in nice suits, helping people in trouble with the law, a divorce or an auto accident. Lawyers had power, that I knew. I saw movies and TV shows about them, but never took particular notice.

By the time we reached our early 30s, now with three kids, our family of five moved to Spokane. A promotion for Michael, but not really what I wanted to do or where I wanted to go. After getting settled and with the kids in school, I found a part-time job as a secretary in a small law firm. I typed, took shorthand, made copies and filed lots of boring papers. Occasionally, I delivered legal papers to the County Clerk's office at the courthouse. While there, I sometimes sneaked into the back of a courtroom where a trial was going on. Watching a live trial was fascinating—much better than Perry Mason on TV.

Opportunities grew for me at the law firm, thanks to the older office manager/secretary who was overworked and stressed out. I learned how to draw up real estate closing papers, instead of merely typing them. I did brief interviews of clients, making detailed notes. I reviewed and indexed medical records for trial preparation. I served legal process papers for which I got extra pay. People got upset when I knocked on the door and handed them a summons or subpoena. Luckily, no one ever shot or assaulted me, even though I heard horrendous stories about threats against "process servers" doing the work I did.

Sometimes I had to gather facts from the Court Clerk's office archived records. I liked interacting with deputy clerks and bailiffs, and they got to know me. In the law office, I became more confident and asked questions about case investigations. Sometimes made suggestions. I slowly absorbed the nuts and bolts of a legal practice, amazed to be paid for it.

As I began to understand this interesting and challenging legal work, I had random thoughts that I could do this—all of it. I saw how things went together and what was needed, even though I struggled with the complicated procedures and legal concepts. I especially liked interacting with and helping clients. Every day was an education.

The lawyers basked in the limelight of the substantive work, collected the fees and got the clients' appreciation. I did mostly grunt work and got paid a pittance. Our office bustled with clients needing help—people injured at work or an auto accident, criminal defendants, employees wronged in their employment, all sorts of disputed contracts. We encountered battered women and desperate housewives needing divorces.

This Spokane firm handled real estate closings, which by law had to be done in a lawyer's office. I became the real estate "closer," having learned to do the title research, prepare the closing papers, interview the parties, conduct the closing conferences, and collect the fees for the law firm. I felt like a hard-working machine on my own, as the lawyer's close supervision became less necessary. I imagined myself as the lawyer, even though that was impossible.

For one thing, my husband and I had three children in elementary school. I had no college degree—only one economics course taken years ago when I had a break after being fired from my job for being pregnant with my second child. Actually, I had been fired from jobs each time I became pregnant. But those are other stories. As for entry to law school, it required an undergraduate degree. I had no degrees, only obstacles, including lack of money for my education. We had no savings for our children's college, much less for me.

I wrestled with my inner thoughts. In an agitated state, I visited the local Spokane community college, then decided to take just one college course that we could afford. Not that I really expected to get very far with one community college course. It was an English literature course—I loved it. My agitation diminished. The following quarter I took a Speech course. My frustrated feelings eased, as I put effort into my classwork.

I worked extra hours at the law firm to pay for the community college courses. I chose classes that would transfer to a four-year university, just in case I ever got there. I didn't dwell on my goals by talking about them. Our family lived day-by-day. I didn't want to rock the boat.

I slogged through long hours of work and study, survived with short hours of sleep. I gradually taught the children how to do laundry, make lunches, do yard chores, take better care of Cinnamon, our sweet Irish setter. I made it a "learning adventure," as if the kids were part of my college work.

They would remind me to get to work on my homework after dinner, as I did with them. We sat at the kitchen table after the dishes were cleared, our homework a jumble of college, middle school and elementary level books and papers. Michael would stand at the sink washing the dinner dishes, amused at our kitchen table disorder. At other times, he and I argued about my time spent and obsession with college courses. He worried a lot about our finances. Michael had his own pressure at the office with all the computer conversions, requiring long hours and overtime. I just kept going.

I took more community college courses—philosophy, history, math, credits that would transfer. I didn't skip summer term. My college credits piled up. I transferred to Gonzaga University as a beginning college junior. By then I had obtained college loans and worked part time at the University Department of Arts and Sciences. Michael became more supportive, yet worried constantly about finances and the uncertainties of my lawyer dreams.

After many difficult stormy conversations with Michael, I went ahead and sat for the LSAT examination required for admittance to the university law school.

After the LSAT results, in a moment of crazy presumption, I proposed to Gonzaga Law School and University that I be accepted into the fall law program before I finished my undergraduate degree in Business Administration/Economics. I proposed to complete my undergraduate degree at Gonzaga while concurrently attending my first two years of law school. I would finish third-year law earning a J.D. with my classmates.

My argument included factors such as the top-notch college grades, my dedication to the university and my "advanced age" (middle thirties), demonstrating my ability and drive to be successful in completion of both college and law school in five years. Juggling class schedules would be a thorny issue, but the proximity of the university campus and law school being virtually across the street, made it seem doable to me. Michael and I both doubted they would allow it. In his words, a "wild ass crazy idea."

I was stunned when deans of both the university and the law school agreed with my proposal. Panic-stricken, I didn't know how I'd be able to schedule undergraduate classes around my rigid law school class schedule, which ended up being the biggest challenge. There was also the problem of my clear breach of historical entrance requirements.

I was strictly warned by the administrators not to publicize this significant exception to law school admission procedures. I agreed to keep the exception secret, and had to sneak around to my undergraduate classes while also attending law school. Since the two campuses were adjacent, I ran back and forth to classes on each campus with extra books in my heavy back pack, powered by my inner excitement. Luckily no law student ever caught on or even questioned my strange unavailable craziness.

The years went by, the money flew out, and our family managed the best we could. Michael and I sold our suburban home and moved to an older modest home in the university district where the children and I could walk to our respective schools. By then, the two older ones were in high school. The move saved time and money, making our lives slightly less hectic. But our household was always frenetic.

In those days, I wasn't home much. Too preoccupied with classes, researching cases, hanging out and studying with new friends. When I did show up at home, my favorite go-to place was a small niche at the top of the stairs, a corner landing with just enough space for a heavy second-hand desk with deep drawers that often got stuck. I had a big old office chair, made for some burly boss man, which I padded with oversized seat and back cushions to make it snug and comfy for me. Next to my chair, a casement window facing the busy Spokane street below offered me a view of traffic and two honey locust trees in the parking strip in front of our house. The white noise of the cars shushing by calmed my distractions and gave me cover.

In the long hours at my desk, I wrestled with esoteric concepts of civil procedure, property, contracts. Legal terms like motions in limine, adverse possession, implied consent. On the wall above the desk, I'd hung a Monet print, "The River," an impressionist image of a woman resting on a river bank, gazing at the still water with reflections of riffled leafy shadows and a faded blue horizon. A breathing muted daydream not fully formed, yet the ethereal image resonated with me. A necessary grounding perhaps.

On the nearby wall, I'd taped current newspaper clippings and photos of Watergate women lawyers in power suits descending the stairs of government buildings in D.C., plus an article and photos of Billie Jean King gloating about her tennis match win over Bobby Riggs. As an emerging feminist in the 1970s, these images gave me a backdrop, inspiration and energy. At my desk, I read, re-read and briefed cases, complied with deadlines, prepared to be called on and humiliated in class by the professor—the battered life of a law student.

A favorite part of my comfy study space was the small window echoing the constant hum of traffic as it buzzed by. The locusts' leaves with their delicate compound patterns and golden chains of blooms fluttered out from the trunk's bulky black bark. They endured the traffic fumes, as I brushed off my own frustrations into the trees' friendly arms—a respite from the printed pages when I got stuck.

The old-fashioned open spindle bannisters that lined the stairway up to my cozy loft also led to the bedrooms and single bathroom for our family of five. Michael and the three kids would file up and down the stairs, usually not interrupting my evening studies. I'd hear their voices downstairs with the TV on, and sometimes catch a whiff of homemade buttery popcorn from the kitchen where the kids did their homework. Hours would go by. I'd forget to get up and move. Michael maintained his tolerant smile. When my younger daughter sat on the stairs reading quietly, I often had no idea she was there.

One evening I struggled over civil procedure, re-reading a case to identify the issue and complex rules. I finally took a deep breath and leaned back in my squeaky old chair, feeling this is just too hard. I sighed and put my head down on my desk as a few tears dripped onto my casebook.

Seconds later I heard a small voice say, "Mommy

can you talk to me now?" I turned around and saw my ten-year-old daughter sitting on the top step of the stairs. I scooped her up and we went downstairs and sat on the front porch together. My guilty heart needed reminders. This was the hardest part.

At the end of my second year of law school, I finished my degree, a B.B.A. majoring in economics. One year later, I received my J.D. degree with honors. Along with a load of student loan debt, no job and lots of uncertainty and fear.

As I look back now, I realize my naivete in assuming that I could simply get out there and "lawyer" just because I had the piece of paper saying I was one. Now in my late 30s, I fretted about who would hire a middle-aged woman with kids. I worried about the burden of student loan debt, not to mention all the sacrifices my family had made. Determined to pay back the student loans as soon as possible, I needed a job offer to show Michael what a great investment these years of chaos had been. I started the job search process.

I wanted a job in private practice doing trial work. I hoped to represent people in legal trouble, get them out of it, and make a decent income in the process. In the days after graduation, I daydreamed about being a successful lawyer. I realized there weren't many women lawyers out there. Our law school class of 175 had only 10% women. But none of that would stop me. At least that's what I thought.

I couldn't help laughing like a crazy woman at times, saying to myself "I am a lawyer" in front of the bathroom mirror just to get used to the sound of it.

In those fearful months before I had a job, I smiled at inappropriate times just thinking of it.

But first I had to walk my naked psyche over the hot coals of the Bar Examination in Seattle for three days in July.

On the first day of the bar exam, I sat down in a cold plastic chair in the Seattle Coliseum filled with hundreds of others. I could smell the desperate fear. Unwelcome thoughts of running away made me grip the desk. I heard only the slight scraping noise of chairs pulling up to the tables. I fingered my thick-shaft pen and twirled it around—a special gift from a fellow student to minimize writer's cramp.

At each place, a stack of empty blue books threatened like an exotic snake coiled to strike. We couldn't touch them until the buzzer sounded. The wall clocks jerked toward nine o'clock, when monitors would distribute the official question sheets. I closed my eyes and silently prayed for inspiration.

As I opened them, a sudden yelp and crash sounded at the table just in front of me. My startled eyes opened wider when the guy on the floor started thrashing, shaking and shrieking. The test monitors rushed over and grabbed him, removing him from the hall, while a nervous murmur arose. An announcement crackled over the loud speakers.

"Everyone—remain in your seats. The bar examination will begin in five minutes."

I closed my eyes again, whirling my pen. The alternating stripes of smooth plastic and soft rubber on the pen felt reassuringly familiar. What was the preface to a seizure? Was I next? My heart kept racing. The student thrashing on the floor made me shake and feel like throwing up. I took a sip from my water bottle. I breathed deeply until the process began again.

Three days of pure hell stripped the stored data in my brain, getting it down in the blue books. I hoped it was the right stuff. My friends and I didn't discuss questions or answers afterwards. That would have been too freaky.

I later wondered what happened to the guy who went to pieces. Someone reported he had a seizure, then saw him back for the second and third days of the examination. I felt my own fear of a seizure lingering under my consciousness for all three days.

Now I had to endure the three-month wait for the bar exam results. Hoping and praying for a job interview and offer in the meantime.

By then, most of my classmates had offers or commitments for jobs. Elite clerkships, public service appointments, plum jobs at desirable law firms, a few as corporate and business counsel. I chose to send resumes only to select law firms, rather than mass mailing. Maybe foolishly so. My goal was to join the combat troop of trial lawyers in the courtroom where the action was. I got routine acknowledgements of my resumes, but no requests for interviews. Finally, I heard from an established Spokane firm of trial lawyers inviting me to an interview.

The day of the interview dawned as a shorts- and-tank-top summer day. I dressed carefully in a lightweight navy-blue linen suit with a subdued ivory blouse, navy pumps and a straw purse with a touch of navy on the trim—my interview outfit. I opened my new black leather briefcase, a gift from my husband on graduation day, empty except for a few copies of my resume. I tried to ignore the wild skittering thoughts in my head as I parked the car and walked to the office building, repeating to myself, "You're fine, you're a lawyer, it's fine." And tried to believe it. I detected dampness under my arms, thankful that my suit was a dark color.

Eager for this interview, I couldn't stop my jitters. I wanted this job. The law firm, like others in the 70s, had no women lawyers.

While I was still muttering affirmations to myself, the elevator doors swished open to the fourteenth floor. A big mahogany reception desk loomed in front of me, the law firm name prominent in shiny letters from the overhead lights. The air felt hushed and close.

"I'm Diana Keatts, for an interview with Mr. Patton."

As I waited in reception, I felt small and awkward, although I'm almost six feet tall in high heels. My legs were too long to sit straight in the soft leather cushions of the low settee. When Mr. Patton strode in to greet me, I struggled to stand up and shake hands. We walked down a long hall past office doors into a corner conference room with a line of full-length windows.

"Sit over here," he said, pulling out a chair facing the light-filled windows.

He settled down across the table, and immediately several men with gray hair filed in and introduced themselves. They selected chairs on Mr. Patton's side of the long polished conference table. Six lawyers in all. Eventually, a young woman peeked in, then closed the door. I didn't expect a group interview. I blinked in the sunlight.

"Okay," began Mr. Patton, "now let's get started. Why don't you tell us why you want to be a lawyer, Diana?"

I recognized my resume in front of him. I smiled and introduced myself again.

"Well, I always wanted to be a lawyer. (Lie) My two uncles are lawyers. (Truth) My parents said I argued a lot." (Truth)

All eyes were on me. I felt like a child who smiled too much, trying to please.

"I'm fascinated with trial work. Loved my trial practice class in law school. I was awarded the top honor for my mock trial presentation." I stopped to catch my breath, not knowing what else to say about that first "why" question.

Another lawyer asked, "Why trial work?"

"Well, uh, I enjoy theatre and had some experience in civic theatre roles. (another stupid Lie) Being in the courtroom is exciting. In a trial setting, you have to understand the law and how it applies to the case. Good communication to the judge and juries means persuasion is important. The courtroom is where advocacy skills matter."

My interviewers listened attentively. Some had furrowed brows with unreadable expressions.

I didn't expect the initial "why a lawyer" question in this setting, even though I've endured that inquiry many times. Didn't these guys already know? After all, they were lawyers. I always stumbled on this question, depending upon who asked and in what context. Maybe I should have said, "Because I know I'm good at it," and let them react. But not in an interview where I was being "proper," trying to impress them.

One of the lawyers asked whether I was married and what my husband did. Was he a lawyer? How many children did I have and how old were they? One man mentioned that the job required out-of-town travel for depositions, interviews of experts, research.

"What would your husband think of you traveling with male lawyers in the firm?"

This caught me off guard. I answered politely, saying that my husband would be fine with whatever the job required. Thinking, why this?

"Who would take care of the children, do the cooking for example, if you were away or working long hours? Often nights and weekends?"

They lobbed these questions in a somewhat friendly inquisitive way as if we were in a social gathering. Like I was a novelty in a cocktail party, juggling answers in a guessing game.

One of the lawyers added, "Well, we haven't had a lady lawyer before, so we're wondering how all this would work."

I smiled again and assured them there would be no problem for my family. I explained that my husband and children already helped with the meals and dishes. That we worked as a team since I'd been in college and law school. My husband liked the idea of a two-income family. I acted agreeable, trying to explain, my politeness feeling forced.

Perhaps I should have shocked them with a wave of my bitchiness, I thought later.

A few questions extended to law school and my intern experience at a Spokane law firm during my last year and a half of law school. I gratefully discussed these topics, working in comments about Law Review participation and my honors at graduation. Then the crusty lawyer with tousled thinning hair at the far end of the table leaned back in his chair and cleared his throat. The way the other lawyers turned to him, he must have been the senior partner.

"Well, what I want to know is who wears the pants in your family?"

I felt a hot flash of adrenaline, paused to breathe, and finally stammered, "I guess we both do." Embarrassed laughter arose from across the table. After that, my mind went blank. My normal breathing resumed only after the interview concluded. Mr. Patton told me he would be in touch. We all shook hands while I forced my thanks with a pasted-on smile. I grabbed my straw purse and brief case, fleeing to the elevator.

Once in my hothouse car parked in the blinding late-afternoon heat, I swore and pounded the steering wheel and swore some more. I flipped on the air conditioner and my body shivered with chills. I was so angry and pissed off, I felt like smashing the windshield. Finally, I could see straight enough to drive home.

In the kitchen after changing clothes, I baked a chocolate cake for our son's birthday dinner. I reported to Michael and the kids that the interview went just fine. That I would hear if I got the job in a few days. It seemed pointless to re-hash the interview or take time out to cry. I didn't want to worry my family.

Later that evening, I gave Michael an abbreviated version of the actual interview. I got worked up again, and Michael hugged me until I calmed down. I didn't understand or expect the interview episode. My focus was getting the job, whatever it took. I couldn't waste time with asshole interviewers dwelling on inappropriate questions.

They rejected me. In the telephone call, Mr. Patton said I was their "second choice." As if that helped. I found out that the job went to someone I knew, a fellow student and acquaintance I had worked with during law school as an intern. Funny thing was, he and I had compared notes about the similarities of our resumes. We had identical undergraduate business/economics degrees from the same university, almost matched grades and honors at law school, both editors at Law Review, plus internship experience. Both in our 30s, although he had military experience before law school. One difference: he was a single male, and I was a married female with children.

I wished him well in the new job. I could not be bitter toward him. I wanted to preserve rapport with my classmate where we continued to work together as law firm interns through the summer after taking the bar exam. I also intended to apply for a lawyer job in that very firm where we were interning. The firm did trial work and valued my research, brief writing and legal analysis. I had helped out in a few minor court appearances on motions. It was a viable future option for me.

By this time, most of my friends had jobs or job offers contingent upon passing the bar exam. Those who could re-locate were on their way out of town. Classmates who vied for clerkships with judges had been selected. Those going into public service awaited their start dates. Many male classmates opted for private practice firms. I didn't have the option of relocating, since my husband was committed to his current employer. I had two more forgettable interviews that went nowhere.

As the summer dragged on, I fretted about student loans, family finances, the job market and rejections. I felt upset, depressed, and out of possibilities. I was choosy at first about my applications, but time was running out. I mulled over the idea of opening my own solo office, but that had its own risks. Not only the initial investment, but startup time and no client prospects. Not a realistic plan.

My application to the firm where I worked as an intern did not work out. Their response discouraged me, especially since they seemed pleased with my work as an intern. They were polite, wished me well, but no job.

In the meantime, the Dean of the Business School at the university needed help. One of the professors suddenly became ill and was unable to teach a class entitled "Business Communications" in the fall term. Would I be willing to fill in as an Adjunct Professor?

The Dean offered to re-schedule the class to evenings to accommodate me. I agreed, realizing that I could teach while continuing my lawyer job search. Teaching the class would be a welcome distraction from the agonizing wait for bar exam results, due out in October.

Chapter 13

Red, White and Blue October

A RED SUNRISE BLAZED AS THE OCTOBER DAY designated for bar exam results arrived. Our study group, comprised of Jack, Patsy, Mona, Josie and I huddled at the university coffee shop. We were fully awake, drinking coffee and eating cinnamon toast. The five of us were close now, with our group study, pre-bar classes, taking the bar, and sweating out the three-month wait. Distracting ourselves by dreams of living a normal life.

Early that red sky morning, we planned to rush the Postal Annex together to search out our bar letters. We couldn't wait around for carrier delivery. The letters would give us the "up or down" on the bar exam results.

Our nervous tics were on full display at the campus cafe. I spilled my coffee. Jack bit his tongue chewing toast. We checked our watches every few minutes, waiting for opening time, so we could walk the few blocks to the Annex.

"If I don't pass, I'm getting drunk even if it's only 9 a.m.," Patsy said.

"Yeah, good. Your house?"

"Calm down, we'll pass," mumbled Josie, her hands twitching as she took tiny bites of her toast.

Finally, it was time to make our death march to the Annex. We all converged at once, telling the postal clerks how important these letters were, like a bunch of crazies who forgot to take their medications. Other classmates were there too. We wanted the clerks to dig through the mail bundles to fish out our Bar Association letters. Since all five of us lived in the University District, we reasoned that the letters would all be in one zip code box. We scribbled down our names and addresses, and showed our I.D.

Even though we were demanding and rude, the postal workers were understanding. This was not their first encounter with berserk law students seeking their bar results. As they searched, we became silent, holding our collective breath. After much sifting through the carrier's delivery bundles, the five letters were found.

Five sets of sweaty hands nervously fingered the envelopes. They felt thick. The clerk who handed us the envelopes smiled.

"The thick ones mean you passed," he said knowingly.

Squeezing our envelopes, we were paralyzed in our eagerness to find out whether we could go on with our lives. Or not. The postal clerks already knew a thin envelope was a one-page notice of failure. They had been through this drill before. The thick ones announced a pass, and contained attachments and forms to fill out for swearing in.

All five of us ripped the envelopes in unison. We stood immobile like statues for a split second. Then jumped up and down screaming until we were asked to leave the building. Our excitement gripped us like winning the lottery. We shouted back our thanks to the workers, as if they were the ones who had passed us. Out on the sidewalk, we re-read the letters of congratulations, the notices and what to do next. Through my blurred vision the words looked like a jumbled heap of scrabble tiles. I felt tears drip off my chin.

We kept shouting, "We passed, we passed, we're lawyers!" Hugging and more hugging.

Anyone who saw us probably thought we were on drugs and needed to be locked up. I can't remember anything about the rest of that day. Except the strange feeling of no more studying, no more exams. Here we were, scruffy law students on the cusp of being sworn in as real lawyers. That was hard to absorb. I ran all the way home to call Michael at his office.

My excitement would have been sweeter if I had a lawyer job waiting, like all my study group friends. All I had was a part-time teaching job as an Adjunct Professor at the Business School. Things looked bleak for me on the job front. The next day I began re-contacting the places I had applied and interviewed, to let them know I had passed the bar exam. Nothing happened.

The following week, the U.S. Attorney James Wilson called to congratulate me on passing the bar. I guess he saw the list in the newspaper. He wanted to know how the job search was going, and I let him know about the rejections.

He asked me to come in to continue a conversation we'd had over a month ago. Our first meeting had been a short chat about his recent appointment as U.S. Attorney by President Jimmy Carter. No hint about any job there. After his second call, my anxiety kicked in again. I couldn't forget my dashed hopes of other interviews, the humiliations of coming in "second."

When I showed up at the U.S. Attorney's office lobby, James greeted me wearing khakis, a casual no-tie shirt and loafers. This interview turned out to be a one-on-one casual meeting with a man whose warmth and sense of humor made me feel comfortable. He wanted to know which firms I applied to and some of the details. I told him the bare bones about interviews.

He made comments about a couple of them. Like, "why would you want to work *there*?" He knew everyone in town.

"Not a single offer from the three-piece-suit lawyers?" he asked.

"Nope."

In his laid-back way of conversation, we talked a bit about politics, local and national. He was a dedicated Democrat, highly involved until his federal appointment. After he was sworn as U.S. Attorney, the federal Hatch Act kicked in, which prohibited all federal employees from participating in political activities. He missed all that.

He asked me about my family, not just about Michael and the kids, but about my parents and my upbringing. I told him about being raised in Chicago, moving out to Seattle in my senior year of high school, my early marriage. I said little about my feat of slogging my way through college and law school in five years.

The interview felt good, a long getting-acquainted conversation. I relaxed and felt more like myself. When I left, we shook hands warmly. He said he'd be in touch.

The next day, he called me to come into the office again. He offered me the job as Assistant U.S. Attorney on the spot. Just like that. No preliminaries. He explained that I had to be cleared by an FBI investigation, involving a lengthy questionnaire, background check and fingerprinting for a security clearance. The details floated above my head. A security clearance and fingerprinting all sounded stiffly official, not even real.

As I left the federal courthouse building, I couldn't keep from dancing. At least that's how my body reacted. A dream job just dropped into my lap. I couldn't believe my good fortune. I raced home with the good news.

Michael was ecstatic to say the least. He told me getting the job was not "lucky," as I kept repeating.

"Diana—look at your long hours, dedication, hard work, almost killing yourself with law school and your business degree at once. This guy James recognizes your potential."

He kept on with a serious recitation of the sacrifices, and I know he meant that for both of us. We sat there as if we were out of breath, holding our grateful hands together for dear life.

His relief was obvious—I would finally earn a salary, after years of incurring debt. My mind ran in circles. I couldn't stop obsessing about the exciting journey about to begin. I changed my clothes to jeans and a tee shirt, then plopped down in a lawn chair in our small backyard of fading fall flowers. The air was clear and breathing seemed easier as I sighed in relief.

My thoughts faded into feelings of gratitude, remembering so many who had inspired and helped me through the peaks and valleys of college and law school. First of all, my long-suffering family.

And of course, the sisterhood of women whose mighty force kept me from going off the track throughout the years.

Chapter 14

Sisterhood

I FIRST NOTICED THEIR OFFICE IN THE HALLWAY near the Spokane County Law Library where I did research for the law firm as a student intern during law school. Their names stood out on the wall next to a nondescript door in the vintage office building:

COLLEEN REILLY and JEAN JENKINS, Attorneys at Law.

As a part-time legal intern, I clocked endless hours in the law library at oversize tables surrounded by mounds of official case law books. A big chunk of my life was spent plodding through complex cases, finding precedent, and crafting background research memos as a basis for the lawyers' trial briefs. I liked the solitary time, searching indexes, analyzing cases, and verifying through "Shepard's Citations" whether the cases were cited further, modified by later rulings, or overturned. Being paid for this important legal work felt good, as I scribbled my findings in endless yellow pages of legal pads.

The day I spied the women lawyers' names on their office door, my curiosity spiked, but I didn't have time to knock or go into their office to find out more.

Not long afterward, our student-run Women's Law Caucus scheduled attorneys Colleen and Jean as speakers, grabbing my attention. The Caucus was an informal group of women law students who got together to let off steam and commiserate about issues of common interest. Things like getting more than one restroom for women in the law school, and how to deal with an annoying male professor who kept calling us "girls" for recitation in class, as in "Let's see, we'll have one of the girls debrief this sex case."

Our Women's Caucus also encouraged female undergraduate students to enroll in law school. Social events at the Caucus were non-existent, because classes, studying, homework and part-time jobs took precedence over almost everything. When Colleen and Jean came to our Caucus meeting, it was our group's best event yet. Our usually bleary-eyed students crackled with energy. We perked up to absorb every word.

Colleen talked about their job searches. We winced as she revealed humiliating experiences like rude sexist questions in interviews and thoughtless turn-downs. Neither Colleen nor Jean got a single job offer, after they had flooded the Spokane market with resumes and endured tortuous interviews.

"So…we opened up our own shop, after much soul-searching. The law school curriculum had no instructions on how to start a law firm, so our efforts became a school-of-hard-knocks education."

"We are both single—no spouses to help out

financially. We borrowed money from our parents, and hung out our shingle," added Jean.

"That was unheard of in those days, at least in our community. Few male law graduates attempted this risky move right out of law school."

Colleen and Jean's gutsy decision stirred skepticism and bemusement. Colleagues and court personnel called them the "ladies' law firm."

At first their office was quiet—not a single client. Their fear pushed them to show up at the local bar association office near the courthouse, hoping that being near other lawyers might bring in clients. They offered pro bono work earning no fees, trying for referrals. They eagerly distributed their business cards to everyone they knew.

"Slowly we attracted a few paying clients—some curious and some in dire need of help. A family friend here, a referral there. Client chairs began to warm up," Jean added.

"We had to minimize overhead. We did the typing, made copies at a local copy shop, and went over to the courthouse ourselves to file our pleadings. We didn't even have funds to hire a law student intern. The last straw, cleaning our office—not what we signed up for," said Colleen.

Colleen and Jean volunteered for appointment as public defenders for indigent criminal defendants in minor cases. They landed two divorce cases. Then lucked out with a personal injury case referred by an insurance agency where Jean had worked part-time in college. They represented a woman who was fired illegally because she was pregnant. A few frantic women with discrimination problems in employment and housing found their way to Colleen and Jean.

"After being in practice for ten months, we finally paid our rent and a few expenses out of our meager income. We were so excited, making deposits of legal fees at the bank. But we were not out of financial straits."

The law students at the Caucus meeting were hungry to learn more. When Colleen and Jean invited us to meet in their law office a few weeks later, we leaped at the chance. While there, we lost track of time and were late to our next class, very noticeable as the women students dribbled in with excitement in their eyes. No comment from the prof that day, but some of the male students knew where we had been.

The following month, our Caucus group showed up again at Colleen and Jean's office with our brown bag lunches to hear more. We sat cross-legged on the floor, since they had few chairs. Being quite mesmerized by these real lawyers, eager to hear all about the nuts and bolts of a lawyer's work, we sat immobile, hardly eating our lunches. Their openness felt comfortable and warm, like loving advice from doting aunts. They looked and talked like us, but with more experience—mentors we could count on.

I thought more about Colleen and Jean, as I lazed in my backyard chair that sweet memorable day in 1977 when James Wilson hired me as a prosecutor in the U.S. Attorney's Office. I remembered about how those informal noon time gatherings morphed into organized support for local women lawyers.

Our meetings attracted more women, although we still sat on the floor with brown bag lunches at Colleen and Jean's office. Eventually they borrowed a small conference room down the hall in their office building at noontime. The sessions evolved into discussions about legal issues and new case law published in "advance sheets," as some of the students passed the bar and became lawyers. We always found time for personal vignettes about local lawyers and judges, listening to each other's stories, courtroom experiences, and dealings with male lawyers.

The women in those groups helped each other grapple with attitudes and incidents that marginalized us. We had concerns about how negative treatment might disadvantage our clients. We offered mutual support, encouragement and criticism. Tears flowed, laughter bubbled. We could be ourselves, out of public exposure. We could discard our "armor" to confront the human issues necessarily a part of practicing law successfully. We marched out of the noon sessions energized with resolve and toughness, our high heels clicking down the marble hallways of the old building, past established law firms that had rejected us.

When I began working as a prosecutor, my courtroom time was almost exclusively in federal court where all the judges were male. I didn't know much about state court judges, except that there were no women trial court judges in eastern Washington. A woman lawyer always came into court as a "lone ranger." Same for attending depositions, arbitration or settlement negotiations. Our sisterhood gatherings with Colleen and Jean became our campfire, our safe place, to help sort things out.

Jack, my good friend from law school, used to needle me about belonging to an organization designated as women lawyers.

"Why on earth do you want to call it a *women lawyers' group?*"

To Jack, our group conjured up tales of male-bashing, or secret stories of a woman's struggle with a male lawyer or maybe some judge's sexual advances. He found our emphasis on women as lawyers contradictory to our goals of fitting into the male world. I told him that as professional women, we felt a unique need to establish ourselves in a legal world dominated by men, and that our sisterhood conversations brought support. He got it, but continued to inquire with a wily grin how the *women lawyers' club* was doing. He was curious, so I decided to invite him to a meeting.

"Do you want to see what goes on?" I chided him at one point.

"Sure, I guess so," he replied. He wanted to.

With a little persuasion, I convinced the group that having a male visit one of our meetings might be interesting. Most of them already knew Jack. By then our meetings spent less time on gender equality issues, and more about positive professional development. We had moved our focus as we gained experience and our numbers increased.

Jack attended two of our noon meetings. After that he never returned except to our social gathering with all the homemade food during the December holidays.

He understood our concerns, but still asked, "Why call it a *women* lawyers' organization? Aren't you trying to be like the men, simply lawyers?"

The thing was, we did feel "different," and had gone through a grueling self-selection process before deciding on our path. Within our lifetimes, women had been excluded from enrollment in law schools and denied the right to practice law. Historically, women were perceived to lack the intellectual gravitas to succeed. Inherent feminine sensibilities were thought to preclude the necessary toughness required of professionals. But as women lawyers, we recognized the importance of our unique experiences and the valuable viewpoints we brought to the table, as well as ways to use these to our advantage.

We forged ahead in our group, tackling worthwhile projects to improve the professional climate for women lawyers. We initiated surveys, authored articles. Grew vocal and creative at addressing gender justice, and developed coping strategies in long, heart-rending sessions. Our collective humor, jokes and self-put-downs kept us from going mad. We puffed up our confidence and celebrated our successes with hugs.

Eventually an official bar-recognized organization, our local chapter of the state Washington Women Lawyers (WWL), grew as more women law students graduated. We took turns at chairing our chapter. Meaningful and effective statewide accomplishments drove the movement forward. High profile women lawyers attracted notice. Nationally, women lawyers gained a foothold.

Sandra Day O'Connor was appointed U.S. Supreme Court Justice in 1981. A year after her appointment, the university scheduled her as a speaker, and our local chapter of WWL hosted a reception before the lecture. Our adoring lawyers' group could not have been more impressed. O'Connor exemplified a lawyer's highest aspiration, and we basked in the golden glow of her appearance.

Washington Women Lawyers continues as a vital thriving organization more than 40 years later. Membership is not gender exclusive. The organization boasts a huge list of accomplishments, including gender-treatment studies of courtroom experience, tracking and support of women judicial appointments, and public recognition of women lawyers' accomplishments. WWL has facilitated women lawyers' seats at the table and the slow process of rewriting the rules.

Colleen Reilly, one of the two lawyers from the "ladies' law firm," became the first female Superior Court trial judge in Spokane County. Others followed in her footsteps. Women judges and justices gradually appeared at both federal and state levels.

While regularly recharging my batteries with the help of other women lawyers, I continued to forge my own path as an Assistant U.S. Attorney. My work expanded to "Lands" cases, which meant representing the government in complex condemnation fights with landowners over value, based on the constitutional concept of eminent domain.

Chapter 15

Condemnations

CONDEMNATIONS IN REAL PROPERTY LAW HAVE nothing to do with hellfire and damnation. The term refers to the land condemnation process by which an owner's land is "taken" for public use by the government, even though the owner objects. In this context, landowners often feel that a government action taking their private property condemns them to hellfire and damnation.

The taking of private property requires that government pay a monetary award of "just compensation" in either a complete or partial taking. This is a special legal process where the amount of "just compensation" is decided. In most cases, the individual and the government agree on the value, ending with payment to the landowner. If there is no agreement, they go to court.

AUSA Rob O'Connor, one of my favorites in the office, introduced me to condemnations.

"These are complex cases that often end up with landowners' very emotional reactions. They resent having their property taken by the government. We get the brunt of it because this creates a wedge between the landowners and us. On top of that, we have to file a lawsuit against the landowner to establish the amount of money the landowner is entitled to, which further antagonizes them."

"Wow, that sounds brutal."

"Yes, and if it doesn't settle, the landowner usually opts for a jury trial—better to have locals on a jury who decide the issue of monetary value because they can identify with the landowner's plight. You know, to punish the big bad government."

"Pretty daunting, I would think."

"In the process, the appraisers for each side evaluate the fair market value of the property taken. Our pretrial work includes investigation, inspection of the property, and discovery which includes depositions of expert witness appraisers," Rob explained.

Rob was a brainy mild-mannered veteran AUSA, known as the "condemnation expert." A short wiry guy, unassuming with a quick Irish sense of humor, Rob chain smoked and had a nervous tic of frequent blinking. The federal government in the 70s and 80s condemned thousands of acres of rich farmland land in eastern Washington. The Bureau of Reclamation appropriated land for irrigation projects and the Bonneville Power Administration (BPA) used grazing land for erection of massive electrical power line towers. Rob was overworked.

After our initial meeting, he handed me the thick U.S. Department of Justice manual entitled "Condemnations" to get started. I wondered how these dry and dull condemnations could ever compare with my juicy criminal cases and complex civil cases with tricky issues, but I soon found out.

My first condemnation trial for the Bonneville Power Administration developed into a many-layered case neither dry nor dull. The government agency had constructed towers and strung electrical distribution lines crossing farms and cattle ranches in southeast Washington near the Tri-Cities of Richland, Kennewick and Pasco. The giant towers and lines allowed landowners to continue ownership and use of their land for growing crops and raising livestock, thus were called a "partial takings." After construction, the government held the right to cross the farmers' lands for periodic tower maintenance.

Rob told me that landowners vigorously opposed the agency's initial condemnation declaration, battling without success. After landowners lost that battle, their antagonism shifted to the issue of compensation, ending up in lawsuits. They hired Seattle lawyers with a reputation as experienced condemnation hotshots.

"Sounds like a lively learning experience," I said.

Rob knew the lawyers.

"This Seattle group are aggressive assholes. They never compromise, give in or give up. You'll see. They thrive on grandstanding for the clients. I got a taste of them during the hearings when the landowners protested the actual takings."

As the court case proceeded, the Seattle hotshots persuaded the judge to allow similarly-affected ranchers to consolidate their cases for trial. They planned for a cadre of angry landowners to inflame the jury because of the government's "oppression."

The trial would occur in the satellite federal courthouse in Richland near the landowners' properties, which would bring a local jury panel sympathetic to the landowners' plight.

Part of the landowners' compensation demands rested on the testimony of expert witness scientists from the East Coast who had studied the adverse effects of power lines' electromagnetic fields on cattle. Effects like diseases and birth defects in the animals' young. We lost our motion to exclude this evidence, even though these novel scientific theories were disputed. Some experts had analyzed the issues and come to significantly different conclusions, finding the research methods and conclusions inherently flawed. We hired those experts to testify for the government.

In addition, the landowners' appraisers presented unorthodox methods for calculating fair market value, turning our established methods on their head.

"The government needs to move out of the dark ages," one of them told Rob and me. He used that same phrase later in trial. These Seattle guys did not let up.

The cases spun out of control, while Rob and I grew dizzy with motions, depositions and calculation surprises in their appraisers' reports. In the process, our government appraiser was entitled to physically inspect the property in the course of preparing his appraisal report.

A date was set for inspection of the largest landowner's property. Rob O'Connor and I accompanied the appraiser and his assistant on the car trip from Spokane to the Tri Cities for the inspection.

"I'm curious to go on the inspection trip, to see the land and the towers, and meet the players."

"Yes, definitely, Diana. And it's a welcome chance to get out of the office and all the stress—a nice change of scene."

On a sunny spring day, the winter wheat fields glowed brilliant green with sprouts like a thick shag carpet. Herds of cattle—russets, ambers, coal blacks with patches of white—munched lazily on sloping pastures in the warm air as far as we could see. On the way, we stopped at a small diner for a quick lunch. Stared at by the locals, the four of us could feel their recognition of us as alien "feds."

Driving out to the property, I nodded in after-lunch drowsiness as we bumped along the country road in a slow lazy rhythm. Our driver turned onto a dirt road uphill to the ranch house. The dusty cloud prickled my nostrils. In the distance, the huge steel BPA structures with multiple crossbeams looked like monster military silhouettes lined up for battle, in contrast to the soft greenness as far as I could see.

Our car bounced over a small rise. A white fence and gate appeared. On the other side stood a handsome white ranch house, a large barn and multiple outbuildings. Sitting in the back seat of the car, I didn't notice a man standing next to the gate until we were right in front of him. He was the property owner, the belligerent leader of the group who hated the government and all its lackeys. Our driver hit the brakes.

"Get off my land or I'll blow your heads off," the landowner shouted as he cocked his rifle, pointing it at us.

I flinched, ducking behind the front seat, trying to shrink as small as possible.

After a long moment, Rob stammered, "Your attorneys gave us permission."

"I don't give a shit. Get the hell out, right now!"

His ruddy face grimaced under his well-worn straw hat. He waved the rifle in small circles. His shirt and jeans threw off particles of dust in the sunlight. He meant business. This was no joke.

Our driver jammed the car into reverse. He managed a U-turn farther down the road. Then picked up speed as we retreated, never looking back. I reeked with fear. Silence hung heavy in the car until we got back to the main road. The appraiser mumbled furiously under his breath.

"How can I do my appraisal without inspection? This is ridiculous. Fucking ridiculous."

We drove directly to the local Sheriff's Office where we reported the incident. Not that anything would ever be done about it, I thought.

Our hope for a pleasant day ended badly. We drove back to Spokane, alarmed and frustrated. When this ugly side of the condemnation case percolated to the surface, I wondered where it would lead. Did we need a U.S. Marshall escort just to inspect the property? Would we need protection at trial?

We did. Rob obtained a court order for the appraiser's inspection. A deputy sheriff and U.S. Marshall later escorted the appraiser to the property. The inspection finally took place without incident. Neither Rob nor I returned to the scene. The landowner was never charged with assault. I worried about what would happen at trial.

The evening before the trial began in Richland, Rob and I went to a nearby pub for dinner with two U.S. Marshalls, Curt Davis and Al Johansen. They were on the scene for the judge's security, to keep order at the courthouse and mostly hang around.

Curt was a tall, bulky, blowhard guy with a big gut, who joked around with a perverted sense of humor. His more serious sidekick Al, with unruly blond hair and a mischievous look, responded to Curt's barbs with more of the same.

Curt would say to Al, "You should show Diana your Marshall's badge…you know what I mean?" They would laugh at their inside joke. It was no inside joke. I knew what they were talking about.

This was the same line Curt had used at the U.S. Marshalls' Christmas party months ago when I'd been cornered by Al and Curt after a few brandy egg nogs. Those conversations were full of playful teasing we all thought was hilariously funny. At some point, Al and I had bumped up against each other, an impromptu flirtation, with some kissing under the mistletoe, a Christmas party sort of thing. We had noticed each other. End of story then.

Back at the pub before the big condemnation trial, Rob and I settled in with Curt and Al, pouring full glasses from pitchers of beer and eating pizza. No worries for me, thinking I had little to do at trial the first day. Rob had the jury selection, opening and initial motions all under control. This was a learning time for me, so I got the easy parts, like examining our expert appraiser later in the week. We relaxed. The guys told jokes and war stories.

Their talk of violence, battles, and destroying the bad guys turned me on. I felt power surges. I was one of the good-guy warriors, picking up the vibes of over-the-edge fury, the taste of victory for its own sake. Winning above all. That's what I wanted, to be like them.

As the night rolled on, Al and I talked on our side of the table about trivial stuff. He had a few funny stories about prisoner lock-ups and weird misunderstandings with witnesses in protective custody, nothing personal. He asked me how I liked my job, and about a couple of criminal cases I had prosecuted. The Marshalls always hung around the courtroom in criminal trials, keeping track of defendants, so Al had seen me in action.

At the table, he moved closer to me. We drank more beer and laughed freely. He looked sexier close up. By the time we left the pub, it was late. Our rowdy little group walked together, Al next to me, back to the motel.

Approaching the motel, he said, "How about walking around the block, get a little air?"

"Okay."

We all said good night, then Al and I walked off. Slowly, because it was dark and there was no sidewalk. He put his arm around me in a protective way. I leaned in. We stumbled a little but it didn't matter. Just kept walking. I felt safe with him.

By the time we got back around the block to the motel, he had a snug hold on me. Things were blurry but I didn't care. We weren't talking much. He ran his hand down my back and around my waist. And back again. We stepped into a full hug and didn't move. He kissed me slowly, then again. Closed his hands around me in slow motion.

"Let's go in," he whispered.

We approached my room. I fumbled with my room key. He took the key and unlocked the door. He stepped into the dark room, pulling me in with his arm still around me. Unzipped his jacket and unbuckled his holster as I watched him. He pushed the door closed, to complete darkness, except for the dim glow from the outside lighting through the thin window drapes shadowing our faces.

Then we stood there, leaning close together for a very long minute. I could feel his heat and my own. He kissed me again and we pressed against each other. His breathing got louder. I felt on fire and kept up with him while we thrashed around.

All of a sudden, I felt a zap of alarm, picturing the courtroom, Rob and I in front of the jury panel coming up the next morning. A wave of sobriety hit me. I took a step back and turned around, feeling woozy and panicked.

Al gradually removed his hands, saying nothing. I backed up further, shaking my head. Very slowly he picked up his holster and jacket. Turned around and left. I closed the door and fell against it for a long time, cooling down. Then I crumpled up in the chair. I couldn't remember whether more happened.

The next morning, I awoke with a jolt under the covers by myself. I lay there trying to stop the pounding in my head. It was dark. The alarm clock hadn't gone off yet. I got up and slapped cold water on my face. Washed down two Advil. Wild thoughts of guilt throbbed through my body, trying to figure out what had actually happened the night before.

Eventually I took a shower, then sat on the bed waiting for dawn, and for the Advil to kick in. In my dazed state, I checked around the room. No gun and holster on the chair. My briefcase and files piled up on the small table. My clothes hanging in disarray in the open closet, my purse open on the floor near the door. Was I losing my mind, my common sense? What was I thinking, or not?

When the morning light came across the window shade, I got up to walk over to the motel's coffee room. Looked around for my room key. Couldn't find it. Alarm bells rang in my head.

I finally opened the door, and there was my room key, dangling in the outside entry keyhole. I pulled the key out, slammed the door and went down to the breakfast room, feeling upset about the night before. My head still pounding.

Rob was already there, his cheery offbeat good humor showing as usual.

"Good morning, Diana."

"Good morning."

"Sleep well?"

"Oh, sure...."

"Don't worry about today, just listen and observe."

A comforting comment, recognizing my hungover look. He had one too, I'm sure, but hid it well. Rob was kind and understanding.

I couldn't get the thing with Al out of my mind. I worried about what Rob thought went on with Al and me. Maybe he noticed the loose key hanging on the outside of my room door. Jeez, what an idiot I am. Paranoia had hold of me.

We sat sipping coffee, companionably quiet. Rob's easy manner made me relax a little.

"Good morning, ladies and gentlemen of the jury. My name is Robert O'Connor and this is Diana Keatts. We're from the U.S. Attorney's office in Spokane...."

The first day of trial was uneventful.

Other than blurting out on the witness stand, "THIS LAND IS MINE," the hothead ring-leader landowner behaved himself. The evidentiary issues had been decided against the government, so the wild west of expert's opinions unfolded before the jury. Rob and I used our wits and proper courtroom procedure. Battle fatigue gripped us as the lengthy trial played out.

The two U.S. Marshalls stood by at attention in the courtroom. I didn't dare look over at them. I knew I would encounter Al again at some point, and that worried me. By now Curt probably had gotten some story or other out of Al about the evening. I tried to flush my mind of all that.

During the weeklong trial, Rob and I had quiet working dinners together, rehashing the day and planning the next. We worked well in a compatible way. No games.

In the end, the jury returned an enormous seven-figure award for the group of landowners, far in excess of our appraiser's testimony and government offers. After the trial, I came to realize the challenges, complexities and high stakes of condemnation cases. High stakes for both the government and the landowners. Not hellfire and damnation, but close enough.

The next week I ran into Al in the courtroom hallway.

"Hi, Al."

"Hey, Diana. Good job on the tough condemnation case."

"Thanks."

I needed to say something.

"Al, last week was way too personal for me…not a good idea."

He gave me a long look before responding.

"I get it. Yeah, Diana. We've got jobs to do, both of us."

I wasn't sure about his reaction.

"I hope you understand."

He finally looked directly at me, winked, said "Sure." We each turned and walked our separate ways.

God, what an idiot I am, drinking too much, then going off taking such stupid risks. I went slowly back to my office trying to calm my jangled nerves. Picked up my telephone messages and a new file that needed attention.

With more condemnation cases, Rob and I became a team as my experience broadened and I felt more confident and grounded. He had me second-chair hearings on water rights cases with him, complicated cases that had dragged on for years, with clashing claims of the tribes, the government and private land owners. These water rights cases with interesting historical aspects never came to trial during my time as an AUSA. But our mutual professional respect and my friendship with Rob flourished.

Chapter 16

Running After Rabbits

When I began my career as a government lawyer, James Wilson warned me.

"This small office covers the entire eastern Washington area from the Cascade Range to the Idaho border. We have only six AUSAs, one located in the Yakima branch office. You will be expected to prosecute criminal cases, defend civil suits, and assist in condemnations. You'll get training at the Department of Justice Trial Institute in D.C., but most of your education will come from the school of hard knocks."

I naively nodded my head. "Okay. I'm so ready for everything out there. I'll work on whatever cases you have." What foolish bravado I had then.

By now I'd survived a few years of the hard-knocks experience. Until one fateful day when I was assigned defense of a seemingly nondescript civil case against the Immigration and Naturalization Service (INS).

The plaintiff was a migrant farm worker picked up by Border Patrol agents in a raid on a central Washington housing camp where workers gathered for dinner with their families. Most were rounded up and forced into buses because of no documentation.

They faced immediate deportation by bus as "illegal aliens" to the Mexican border near Tijuana.

One of the Hispanic workers, a U.S. citizen, objected to being grabbed in the raid, even though he was eventually released. He looked up the local public Legal Services office to see what his rights were. This worker became the plaintiff in the civil rights case which disputed the "illegal search-and-seizure violations of constitutional and civil rights by the local Border Patrol agents and officers, including liability of their INS superiors in Washington, D.C."

In reviewing the case, I talked with Border Patrol agents and their local INS supervising officer. According to them, their actions in the migrant worker camps and deportation of the illegal aliens were carried out strictly in accordance with INS rules and regulations. The agency had been conducting these raids for years and never been questioned, they informed me.

Agents told me that gathering up and deporting the illegal workers was a never-ending process. Often the same workers would be found and sent back to Mexico several times in one agricultural season. They gave an example of one Mexican worker.

"The wetback took his old car into a shop to be repaired, then was deported on a Friday. We heard he picked up his car at the shop the following Tuesday."

"You mean the same guy showed up in the same town in rural Washington state four days after he'd been deported?" I asked.

"Yep."

The INS agents thought this rather laughable. Some sort of game.

I thought about their INS game being played with people's lives. These civil procedures seemed pointless—and heartless. Government agents and resources were used to disrupt these workers and their families' basic existence. The people weren't criminals. They just wanted work to support themselves and their families. Yes, they were in the U.S. illegally, a civil offense, during the agricultural season after which many returned to Mexico for the winters. I wondered about the relevance of constitutional restraints on criminal search and seizures. Were they in play here? A bunch of questions prickled me. But I didn't argue or vent my personal concerns to the INS. Not at the beginning.

The official deportation statistics charted the many thousands deported each year. The agency justified its budget and fulfilled its mission. The agricultural employers, though sometimes temporarily inconvenienced, had access to docile, cooperative workers. Crops were well-cared for and abundant. The wealthy farmers and food processors banked the profits.

This civil rights lawsuit was a small annoyance to the INS at first. Except shortly after the suit was filed, a motion was made by plaintiff's attorneys to certify the case as a class action on behalf of all agricultural workers in eastern Washington whose civil rights had been or might be violated as a result of the raids by the INS agents both in the fields and migrant housing areas.

The public interest legal services group which represented the plaintiff contended that the raids amounted to criminal arrests, thus subject to constitutional scrutiny under the Fourth Amendment prohibiting search and seizure without probable cause. The motion for class action certification was supported by affidavits and lengthy legal briefs. Their passionate arguments were based also on public policy grounds, the "moral authority" rationale that is sometimes devalued but can be persuasive. The issue had potentially far-reaching implications for the INS, their policies and practices. The complex lawsuit escalated, attracting the attention of higher ups in government as well as the press.

I spent an increasing percentage of my time and energy defending the case on various fronts. The underlying constitutional challenges to longtime INS policies and practices were especially worrisome and allowed for broad pretrial discovery by the plaintiffs' lawyers. The D.C. immigration bureaucrats held lengthy meetings with local agency heads.

Border Patrol agents hung around my office, insisting that the lawsuit was frivolous. They expected me to make it disappear, arguing to me they had been doing their immigration sweeps always following INS standard operating procedures. Because the INS deportation process was governed by INS civil regulations, no one had given any serious thought to the possibility that the raids resembled criminal arrests or might be subject to constitutional search and seizure scrutiny. Basic criminal procedural law didn't fly as a red flag on their radar.

Ned Buck, one particularly outspoken Border Patrol

agent, argued with me frequently.

"These wetbacks are here illegally. Our job is to round them up for deportation. We follow the written procedures of the D.C. manuals. Period. What more are we supposed to do?"

I explained the potential constitutional problems with the lawsuit as best I could. But many of the agents had a chip on their shoulders about their work being called illegal. They blamed me for not getting the case dismissed promptly. Ned continued his defensive harangues.

"You have no experience with this stuff. We're being hung out to dry. Why should we have to answer questions in depositions and all this other bullshit?"

I patiently explained the procedural aspects of the case to Ned and the others, about how it takes time and court hearings to set up defenses to support motions to dismiss. Tried to impress on the agents the breadth of the lawsuit and the ramifications of class action certification if the court allowed it. Their puzzled hostility toward me continued, as it became evident that they probably didn't like a woman representing them. After all, these macho guys enforce immigration laws and keep citizens safe. I had to keep my cool and discuss the issues rationally as their lawyer, which apparently was not enough.

I moved forward within the Federal Rules of Civil Procedure, even though at times I was outmaneuvered and humiliated by the plaintiff's lawyers. I kept my game face on, even though my inner confidence waned.

"You aren't making any progress. We're the ones being harassed. You don't have the background or know what's going on," one vocal agent complained. I referred him to the D.C. immigration attorneys I was working with. This continued criticism from the agents was getting to me.

As I assembled investigative information, affidavits and legal research for the official response to the Motion for Certification as a Class Action, I doggedly pursued questioning the agents about specific details of their procedures. They resented my pushy grilling.

During one of these conversations, the agent-in-charge of the local office suggested that I accompany the agents on one of their raids. The agents were convinced that I would learn from watching one of their actual "field trips." They wanted to show their operations as humane, orderly and effective. In short, "lawful," as in accordance with regulations. I agreed to participate as an observer in a field raid.

On a late spring day, as a passenger in the car of local INS Supervising Agent Randy Arnsforth, I was to observe the Border Patrol operations in central Washington's lush agricultural areas irrigated by Bureau of Reclamation projects. When we arrived in the general vicinity, we gathered at the local INS office to coordinate plans for later that day. About ten agents and numerous vehicles were already lined up. Agents were armed and their large unmarked dull-green vehicles were equipped with metal screens behind the driver's seats.

In late afternoon, the uniformed agents were

ready to roll. As I rode "shotgun" with Randy, in the rear of the group, I didn't have a clear view of the agents in front. We drove through orchards, wheat fields and acres of hops fields. Hops fields are labor intensive, requiring hand-stringing and gentle touch to attach the vines to the poles. It was the hottest new cash crop.

As we approached, the workers were visible, some on ladders working with the poles and twine. Suddenly, I saw a wave of movement. The workers drew together and disappeared over the horizon in unison, like a flock of sheep being herded in for shearing.

Randy clued me in, "See, they know our vehicles, they're all starting to run."

He quickly braked and jumped out of the car, shouting, "Follow me."

Randy, with his long legs, ran across the hops fields over field poles and strings on the ground. I could hardly keep up in my tennis shoes, trying to avoid catching my foot on a line or pole. Every now and then the agent would turn around to see that I was in his shadow. We ran for what seemed a long time. I was out of shape and out of breath.

Most of the agents were ahead of us, dashing after the fleeing workers. As Randy ran, he turned and yelled, "Watch the rabbits run!"

I felt pressure to keep up with the chase. This was exciting, like being in an adventure movie except it was dead serious. Eventually we arrived at a group of collared workers being herded by the agents into a space near the busses.

Showing sad sullen expressions, most of the captured had their hands in the air. Two large busses appeared which had been parked in the eventual path of the running workers, on the opposite side of the open fields from where the agents began the chase.

Randy told me the prisoners were being processed. I could hear the Spanish-speaking agents talking and the workers responding quietly. One by one, they were pushed into a bus after the agents filled out paperwork on clipboards. The agents kept me away from the processing.

The agent-in-charge whisked me behind the vans, and one of his subordinates brought the car over for Randy and me to leave the scene. He drove in silence at first, then wanted my feedback.

"Well, what did you think?"

I didn't have a ready response.

"I've, uh, never seen anything like this. I'll have a few questions for later. I'm exhausted."

On our way back to town, Randy and I saw an older Hispanic-appearing man raking a yard of a big house.

I said to Randy, "What about him?"

The agent stopped and asked the man in Spanish for his papers. The man shrugged and looked dejected. The agent put him in the back seat and they conversed in Spanish. Randy spoke to him, then they collected the man's wife from a small shack in back of a nearby house. We drove them to the buses. On our way back in the car, Randy explained that the man told him the couple wouldn't return again because they were too old, after being deported several times.

I had a sharp pang of guilt. Why had I spoken up about this man doing yard work peacefully in someone's yard just because he looked Hispanic? I felt sorry for the old couple and wished we had let them go. But I said nothing, just sat there feeling sad and mixed up. Was I just as cruel, complicit in this operation? I pushed aside my feelings, which was my self-preservation routine in those days. I had my job to do, so kept blinders on for my own peace of mind.

When we returned to the motel, Randy pointed to a little café next to the motel where I could get some dinner, and said we'd meet in the morning for breakfast before we drove back. As I got out of the car, he reported that they had "captured almost 60 wetbacks in the raid," a respectable number for the day's effort. He said the agents would meet after everyone was processed and sent off on busses. I was not included in their after-raid debriefing. Randy said "off the record" that there would be drinking and the guys could get kind of crude.

"No need for you to be there. So…see you tomorrow morning," he called as he drove off. I pushed my imagination out of focus.

That evening while I ate a quiet dinner by myself at the café, I wondered how the agents were feeling. Was it a celebration after the hunt? Was it a body-count of the "rabbits" caught? I felt downcast at how the Hispanic workers were chased like animals. Open hunting season on them. Catch and deport. Never mind the workers' families, and whatever pay might be forfeited. They were rounded up and returned to Mexico—mere statistics on the INS weekly reports.

Was I aiding and abetting?

As we drove back to Spokane the next day, Randy explained how the operation had gone well, all according to plan, following INS procedures. How the hard-working and conscientious agents caught and deported a large number of illegal aliens, which was their mission. He emphasized that agents usually round up the aliens in the fields and not at their worker housing. According to Andy, "that happens rarely."

But it certainly had happened in the housing camps in this case I was defending.

I didn't have much to say, since I wasn't there to justify their methods, only to observe. They wanted approval, which was obvious from their attitude about their operations. I felt reluctant to pass judgment, realizing I needed more time to analyze what had occurred yesterday in the hops fields. It appeared that they had followed published procedures, conducting the raid to fulfill the INS stated mission. They hadn't roughed up or mistreated anyone that I could see.

I couldn't talk about my conflicted feelings with my colleagues, since I was expected to be a hard ass prosecutor/defender. In this case, that was my sole job: to defend the INS and resist the Motion for a Class Action.

To obtain the court's approval of the case as a Class Action, the plaintiffs' lawyers argued that the suit was brought on behalf of other persons similarly situated, and that the case raised common issues of law and fact. Thus, the court should decide one consolidated case on behalf of the group rather than deal with multiple individual lawsuits.

In pretrial discovery, many depositions were taken, documents requested and written interrogatories posed to the government. Most discovery was instigated by the public interest law firm, which was committed to the undocumented workers who had complained of the objectionable behavior of the INS for years.

I defended the government's actions with facts, law, official regulations, as well as testimony by the agents whom I got to know over time.

Most of them were responsible likeable guys, familiar with their mission. Some had a self-righteous attitude. A few had chips on their shoulders with a "Rambo" attitude. Those were the ones who needed lots of preparation for their depositions. In our office conversations, the term "wetback" was used freely by some agents. I told them flat out they were not to use the derogatory term in their depositions. I let them know it was not a good idea to use it anytime. That caused resentment with some agents since this term was an accepted part of their "lingo."

A few of them found it hard to remember to avoid the term wetback when the depositions heated up, as they often did. The agents managed not to speak the word aloud, so it did not show up in the transcripts, but I detected the unspoken word on their lips more than once. The term "wetback" came from the demeaning reference to those who entered the U.S. by swimming across the Rio Grande River. Not acceptable in our setting, or anywhere else for that matter in my book.

When I was in D.C. for depositions of the Director and deputies of the Immigration Service, they had taken increased notice of the eastern Washington lawsuit. The higher-ups disliked testifying, especially being pushed to justify their regulations. The plaintiffs' lawyers put INS officials on the spot with accusatory questions about separating families, entering housing areas without a search warrant, and about workers' lost pay when captured and deported. The constitutional questions and issues were key, and the plaintiffs' lawyers were tough, competent and persistent.

The U.S. District Court eventually granted certification of the class action, with the substantive claims to be decided in a later hearing or trial. A Motion for a Restraining Order pending the final resolution of the case against the INS was filed with the court, on the basis of illegal search and seizure practices and procedures. All hell broke loose in D.C.

The plaintiff's argument alleged that the raids were, in essence, criminal arrests, and thus subject to Fourth Amendment constitutional restraints, meaning that probable cause that a person was in the U.S. illegally must be required for a "stop" or "arrest." Therefore, someone could not be stopped merely because of brown skin or Hispanic appearance. With this motion pending, delays and continuances prolonged the case.

While resisting the class action case, the INS contemporaneously began to modify internally its actual practices of random raids of fields and worker housing. The INS hoped or imagined that the case would fade away if enough time elapsed and procedures were informally changed by the INS itself.

By this time, some Department of Justice attorneys in D.C. were actually managing aspects of the case because the INS was freaking out about ramifications to their nationwide policies and procedures. Even though they began to revise their written procedures, INS would not agree to allow the court to enter a Consent Decree or any compromise settlement. They refused to be forced by court order to change, and thus be subject to penalties for noncompliance. The case had now dragged on for over a year.

When the Motion for a Restraining Order and Permanent Injunction was eventually granted by the court, the plaintiffs became the "prevailing parties" according to federal statute. The government was ordered by the court to pay all the legal fees and costs incurred by the plaintiffs. The amount paid to the public interest law firm was substantial. Years later, an agreed Consent Decree was entered in court, after I had left the U.S. Attorneys' office for private practice.

When I think about this INS case of decades ago, I remain amazed at the stubborn resistance of the INS to change its policies. The posture of the government was singular: to resist and defend. Pressure, expense and legal maneuvering do not easily move a massive government agency which does not relish supervision by the courts. As the government's lawyer, I had little discretion since the Department of Justice and the INS dictated policy, even though I felt sympathy for the plaintiffs' arguments on behalf of the workers. My conflicted feelings left me stressed and split into pieces. This was one of the factors that eventually led me to consider leaving government service to join a private law firm.

"Running after rabbits," chasing the "wetbacks" and "illegal aliens" stuck in my mind. I carried with me lessons learned, like the stark realization that deep personal feelings can make lawyering a complicated business. One that left me feeling compromised and anxious.

Yet I always knew as a government officer or as a private practice lawyer, being an advocate carried certain duties. Which meant that when I agreed to represent a client, I had to be all in. My professional responsibility required me to obtain the best possible result within ethical standards. If I could not do that, I had to withdraw from representation. Not as easy as it sounds.

My thoughts about private practice continued, even though I didn't have time to do anything about it, always up to my armpits in demanding lawsuits and prosecutions for the government. Until I received a telephone call from a former boss.

Chapter 17

Token Woman

WHEN I FINALLY TOOK TIME TO CONSIDER JOINING a private law firm in 1981, public perceptions of female lawyers had evolved from my law school days. Broad cultural attitudes about women working "outside the home" reflected increased tolerance and acceptance. More women became visible as practicing lawyers, which gradually affected local attitudes.

For example, Spokane attorneys Colleen and Jean had moved along in their private practice. They showed up regularly in courtrooms, bar association functions, and other lawyers' offices for depositions and consultations. At the law school, a female professor taught complex contracts classes with a competent and gutsy attitude. Another taught a first-ever class, "Sex Based Discrimination," using a textbook written by Ruth Bader Ginsburg who later became a Supreme Court Justice. Local reporters, curious about the "female prosecutor," followed me around at the courthouse, sat through a few trials, and would name me as the prosecutor in occasional clips about ongoing trials.

People actually showed less astonishment when encountering me as a lawyer. Women lawyers, including myself, relaxed their guarded ways. I didn't forget, but quit dwelling on previous stuff that had demeaned me as a professional woman.

In this changing milieu, Fred Jones, the managing partner of the law firm where I had interned while in law school, called me out of the blue.

"How about getting together for coffee," he said, after we had chatted politely. I wondered what he was up to. Neither of us would have chosen the other for a coffee mate.

We chummed up at a local coffee shop, and settled down with our coffees and generalities. He casually inquired whether I had considered going into private practice. I shrugged. The question was an unexpected twist from our long-since severed relationship. Back then, I had applied eagerly for a lawyer job at Fred's firm in the summer of the bar exam, but was rejected as another "second choice." The queasy ripple of rejection roiled in my stomach, as I remembered the turn-down. I put away memories of my frustration over that episode, and sipped my coffee.

Fred brightly recited a few highlights of my past few years as a prosecutor, noting two criminal convictions profiled by the press. Using flattery to soften me up.

"You've done very well," he said. "I've heard from a couple of lawyers you were up against. Sounds like you're pretty tough."

I smiled. Waited for him to stop the bullshit and get to the point.

More small talk, then Fred asked me again about going into private practice. More specifically, joining his firm as a trial lawyer. His prominent firm's top-notch lawyers were well-heeled and well known, with an impressive book of institutional clients. He had my full attention by then, prodding me with his persuasive jury trial demeanor.

"We'd really like to have a woman in the firm, and that woman is you, Diana."

I listened without reaction as he droned on with more of his patronizing.

"Will you think about it?" he pressed.

My cynicism melted. The prospect of joining his prestigious firm tempted me. Challenging civil litigation and the opportunity to work on complex cases with lawyers at the top of their game sounded pretty exciting. I figured that the salary and bonus potentials weren't bad either. Fred didn't quote numbers, but I knew there would be more money in private practice than I earned as a government lawyer. He also mentioned the possibility of becoming a partner "if it all worked out." He dangled vague promises like a devil with a pot of golden coins. His cheery confidence spoke like the wily lawyer he was.

As we left our lengthy tete-a-tete, Fred said that he wanted me to meet with the firm partners to discuss details of an offer.

"Fred, this is a lot for me to think about. I need to discuss it with Michael."

"Sure, sure, I understand. Take your time, Diana."

As I walked back to the federal building alone, I felt

a glow of satisfaction floating around me. Fred and his firm had noticed my hard work, my accomplishments. The unexpected approval circled me like a warm generous hug. But there were rough edges to it.

I forced myself into a reality check that evening, as I told Michael about Fred's offer.

"Hiring a woman is becoming a popular thing. They could show me off as their woman lawyer. Appear modern and tolerant. Non-discriminatory."

I told Michael that I hoped that male professionals, especially the older ones, were coming to realize that female lawyers were a lot like them. Pursuing similar goals, like meaningful work for a decent salary.

"Did he mention salary specifically?"

"No, but vaguely mentioned partnership in the future."

"That sounds good."

I got stuck on Fred's specific words repeating that they wanted to hire a *woman* lawyer. The more I said that out loud, the worse it sounded.

"Michael, I feel labeled for something I have no control over—my female gender."

"Well, maybe they think a feminine name would stand out on the letterhead for clients to see. Increase visibility and attract certain clients."

"They obviously want me to fill a specific role. Since I've proved myself in the courtroom, they *finally* feel I'm a known quantity, a safe hire. They could market my federal court background. I can see where they're going."

"Well, yeah, and be recognized as an experienced lawyer. Work on good cases." Michael looked at the positive.

"This is too much to figure out in one night." I started fixing dinner.

Michael poured me a glass of wine, and I starting chopping vegetables for a salad. He put his arms around me and said "you know you're good—don't settle for less than what you want."

I agonized over my conversation with Fred and his firm's interest in me. The splendid opportunities and perks attracted me to a desirable professional lifestyle. As an obsessive courtroom lawyer, I loved civil litigation cases. I weighed my pros and cons, wavered back and forth. Discussed the options endlessly with Michael until we were exhausted, even though I hadn't received a salaried offer yet.

In the end, I couldn't shake memories of my history with the firm. Like Fred's criticism of me as a *female* intern sent to traffic court, getting a bad result even though expected. His insulting "body shop" talk describing Claire and me as we worked as law students in the firm library. Lesser slights ignored and mostly forgotten. These uncomfortable echoes worked as background noise warning me about the prospect of joining the firm.

"Michael, I just don't feel right about Fred's firm. Too many concerns I can't ignore."

"I get that. This thing about hiring you just because you're a woman is a bad sign. But, think about it, that could pass. When they see the quality of work you're doing."

"Yeah, I know."

"Diana honey, it's really your decision. You're the one who has to work there."

I finally decided to reject Fred's offer, careful not to burn bridges. But the prospects of private practice triggered realizations about my accomplishments so far, and what they meant for my future.

On the professional stage while in the U.S. Attorney's office, I purposely avoided showing up as an ardent feminist who mouthed off at every perceived insult. My approach was a quiet struggle to overlook the unexpected slights. I strove for effectiveness to maximize my professional role and force myself to focus. It kept me from crying. Or laughing at the comic side of serious issues.

In the process, I was thought to be more placid than I actually was. My practiced lack of reaction to slights protected my psyche. I approached my work with fierce determination, displaying my sense of irony, annoyance or humor only when I felt secure. My defensive perfectionism created success. I never lost a single criminal case that went to trial. I ran full speed ahead to exceed expectations.

The never-ending hours of preparation and strategy while constantly being "on" in the courtroom took its toll which I refused to admit. I forfeited vacations, social events and other pleasures in life. It was a mad juggle between Michael and me. Although it sounds strangely basic, the tactile routine of cooking dinner at home when I was in town was a great stress reliever. For both of us.

Michael and I agreed that a transition to private practice should not happen simply because I was sought after primarily as a *woman* lawyer. There was more at stake.

"Don't be a token hire, Diana. You know you're a first-rate, experienced lawyer. Period. Make them want you for that."

He was right of course. I expected to be recognized as an experienced competent trial lawyer. Going into private practice, I needed to match up with a firm where I would flourish professionally and everyone would benefit. Besides, I'd been hired as the "token woman lawyer" once already, although I was still unsure about why I was chosen right out of law school to work as a federal prosecutor. Nevertheless, my federal practice had been spectacular in so many ways. Now I had a fat resume with options.

I continued to hone my trial skills while working on my pending federal cases. Yet in the back rooms of my mind, ambitions about private practice simmered.

Chapter 18

It's A Wrap

In the meantime, the pressure of the sprawling Immigration class action lawsuit aggravated me as it heated up. With my sporadic concerns about the plight of the Hispanic workers, the burden felt heavy. I was on the wrong side. My heart wasn't in it, although I held my tongue with the powers-that-be in Washington D.C. and with the agents in Spokane.

To top it off, I had suspicions about the potential for collusion between the farming employers and the government agents. The farmers, ranchers and related businesses in central and eastern Washington state pocketed millions from the abundant well-tended crops. Apples, pears, cherries, peaches, peas, corn, potatoes, grains and sugar beets produced record harvests. The acreage for lucrative hops crops increased at a record pace with abundant Hispanic workers who provided hands-on labor for setting lines and poles, and harvesting of the delicate hops flowers used for making beer.

Of course, the agricultural employers disliked interruptions caused by the INS periodic capture of their workers. These workers were cooperative, hard-working, and eager to earn whatever wages they received. Because of fear of deportation, they kept together and lived under the radar. On the other hand, the employers may have gained financially when wages weren't fully paid because employees were grabbed by the Border Patrol agents and deported. Was it a coincidence that the raids occurred late in the day or week? I suspected that employers had some inkling of timing of the raids. More money in the employers' pockets, if workers missed a paycheck.

The dehumanizing aspects of the raids made me want to talk to James Wilson, my boss, about my concerns. But I was reluctant in light of my heavy responsibility as the local AUSA defending the INS. I couldn't risk my required loyalty, nor could I withdraw from the case.

As I was feeling a crisis of conscience over my defense of the Immigration case, another class action arose. A sex discrimination case by women employees of the Department of Energy (DOE) at the Hanford nuclear site in Richland, one of the Tri-Cities in southeast Washington. The lawsuit claimed that the DOE failed to promote qualified women into management, and that the agency's actions constituted a nationwide systematic pattern and practice of violations of Title VII, the federal law against discrimination.

This new lawsuit had the potential to explode into a giant case against the U.S. Department of Energy because they contended that the named plaintiff and other similarly-situated women employees constituted a "nationwide class." The process of class action certification would be lengthy and tortuous, probably involving statistical experts battling over opinions and conclusions after the discovery process. The government would be required to produce voluminous files and records.

I was assigned to defend, in coordination with attorneys at Justice in D.C.

The first thing that struck me was the irony of my role on the defense. Not only ironic, but personally distressing. No time for pondering however, as I had work to do. Enter a Notice of Appearance, coordinate with the DOE in Richland, and immediately visit the officials at DOE and Justice in D.C. Prepare for an onslaught of discovery requests that were sure to come.

The plaintiffs were represented by Seattle's top-notch employment discrimination litigators, headed up by a ferocious lawyer by the name of Elizabeth Branson. I'd never met her, but knew of her fierce advocacy on behalf of women. Elizabeth was an active member of the Washington Women Lawyers network. She also participated in governance for the state Bar Association, a very public role.

When I told my friend Josie about the sex discrimination lawsuit and my responsibilities to defend, that got her attention. She listened intently, then sat up straight, wide-eyed.

"No shit, this is incredible. Does the case have merit? Sounds pretty plausible."

She raised her eyebrows, wrinkling her forehead in her wise-woman way, as we both had preconceived ideas about the likelihood of merit in these types of claims.

"I haven't seen any hard data yet, only the named plaintiff's employment records. Which don't tell the whole story."

"Diana, this could put you in a very dicey role to say the least. What's next?"

"I go to D.C. I'll work with DOE and Justice attorneys to get a bigger picture about the initial issue of class certification."

"Sounds like a pretty big fucking deal, and maybe public attention. Are you ready for that?"

"Well, things keep getting more complicated and overwhelming."

I sighed, thinking how I hate ambivalence. Premature public scrutiny is very difficult. This case could be nothing but trouble.

Josie and I sat in a corner of our comfy out-of-the-way coffee shop, sighing over this latest development. My head was going in circles.

"I am thinking ahead to possible merit to the plaintiff's claims and what might happen to my representation of the DOE."

"Yeah, that would be a dilemma for sure. What about settlement?"

Josie could cut to the chase.

"Then I'd have to assemble the evidence and talk seriously with the DOE powers-that-be. Which scares the hell out of me. I have more than enough tension and stress going on with my other class action, the immigration case."

"Geez, Diana, sounds like a shitload. So much time in D.C. and all over the country these days."

"Yeah, and Michael's getting more out of sorts when I'm out of town. Halfway pissed off all the time."

Josie knew Michael and I had issues going on. She looked at me, like how serious is this stuff going on with you two?

"Me and Michael…kind of off on our separate tracks. He's busy with computer conversions and all his brainy assistants. One spends a lot of time with him. He says she's a real crackerjack figuring out the complicated computer programming and systems problems."

"Hmmm."

She got it. I didn't want to tell her all the specifics about Michael and me. I needed to change the subject.

"So, Josie, how's it going with your public defender gigs?"

"Yeah. Well, lots of interesting clients and cases. I'm now in the official listing for public defender appointments for Superior Court. Finally."

"Wow, that's great."

She was tough, down to earth, and clients accepted her practical advice. Josie worked well with the state prosecutors and knew how to plea bargain. She was making a name for herself.

I let her know I hadn't ruled out jumping ship at the USA's office for private practice, even though I had no plan or timeline. Josie was always good for pragmatic advice and encouragement.

"Maybe you need to look more broadly. What might be out there in the private sector. You're a hot commodity by now. Think it over."

It helped to talk things over with Josie. It made me sort things out, rather than avoiding the hard issues in my personal life. My tendency to forge ahead without counting the cost to myself and especially to Michael, could be a disaster if I didn't slow down.

I spent time mulling over my options. Michael and I had endless conversations about timing a move to private practice. He disliked that I was overworked, constantly out of town, spread too thin, and often too busy for time together. My efforts on the two dominant cases, the immigration lawsuit against the INS and the discrimination case against DOE, required massive hours. Even though the INS case was winding down to some extent, the court rulings and compromises angered INS people, both in D. C. and Spokane. In both cases, I had to suppress my instincts in order to follow DOJ protocol because they wanted aggressive action, not philosophical musings. This lack of clarity in my work caused sleeplessness, feelings of inadequacy and sudden bursts of internal anger. I was cranky and distracted. Michael was becoming distant.

I continued to defend the two cases at full speed, but the stress of it all made me feel uneasy and unsure. Then I'd go home and talk to myself, argue and overthink the issues. Remembering that I was just doing the job as directed by my U.S. government employer—my ethical duty, so why fight it?

No, it was more than that to me.

I needed to talk with my boss James Wilson, about my concerns. I suspected he might listen, maybe sympathetically. Or, maybe not so much, and loyalty issues would arise.

In those years while I worked with him as the U. S. Attorney appointed by President Carter, I got to know James in bits and pieces. A slightly scruffy guy with an odd edge, I could see he was a renegade from the start. I surmised he had hired me on a whim after learning the "three-piece-suits" in private practice rejected me. He may have thought I was also an outlier, a contrast to the career prosecutors in the office. I found out later that the Carter administration had quietly hired significant numbers of women and minorities in D.C. and certain U.S. Attorneys followed suit. I felt lucky when hired, not questioning why.

James gave a first impression of my own disheveled middle-aged uncle who didn't give a damn about conservative norms or protocol. I couldn't forget the off-the-wall flag salute incident my first day as a federal prosecutor. I never figured out whether James was aligned with some Vietnam vets for peace who refuse to salute the flag as a symbol of our nation's reckless proclivity to wage war, or whether he was just weird. I should have spoken up or asked questions, but never did because of my puzzled embarrassment.

James was unpredictable, hard-to-read, gruff in a kindly way, distant yet warm. Funny to the point of hurtful sarcasm. He played practical jokes that made people furious. Like the time he barged into my office to ask if I had a flask of spray perfume in my purse, as women did in those days.

"Give it to me," he said.
"Why?"

"I'll tell you later."

Not knowing what to do, I dug in my purse and handed it to him. I found out days later he had sprayed my perfume on a male intern's sports jacket hanging in the hallway. The intern had just announced his engagement. I never heard anything about his fiancee's reaction when the intern got home from work that night. A warped sense of humor and rather cruel, I thought.

James' practical jokes and unpredictable behavior contrasted with his concern for the disadvantaged. That part of him wasn't out in plain sight, but occasionally his preference for the underdog became public. Like his determined involvement in prison reform for violations of civil rights in the state prison in our District. He hired a firebrand woman lawyer from D.C. Justice on temporary duty to pursue the claims, creating a lot of dust and push back.

Anyone who worked with him had to notice James' oddball personality traits. Although he infuriated me at times, mostly he left me alone, let me do my job and didn't interfere with my prosecution declinations or try to run my cases (except for my child rape case), especially after I had been there awhile. I felt he wanted me to succeed, to find my way.

That didn't mean he was open with me. I was still wary, not able to gauge his reactions which could be volatile. If I frankly revealed my concerns about the immigration and the sex discrimination cases, it could be risky. He was an enigma, and my protective armor kept me silent. Especially while I was considering a change to private practice.

I quietly pursued my search for a law firm with lawyers I could work with and a practice that suited my skills and desires. My thoughts included the pragmatic, plus considerations of my personal life. In private practice, I imagined some control over cases I handled, a lower stress level, less public exposure and a higher income. I'd be in town most of the time. That would mean dinner at home, knocking off the heavy drinking, and improvement in Michael's and my love life that had gotten off the track. More time for us together.

I contacted some law firms through friends and colleagues, and applied to a few in a covert way so as not to alert my fellow AUSAs. The process and interviews went significantly better than my initial job interview process during the summer of the bar exam. I didn't encounter the "why a lawyer?" question even once.

I eventually accepted an associate position at an established firm of lawyers, all interesting and friendly men of mixed ages, representing a vibrant assortment of clients and litigation striking the right chord from the beginning. I was excited about the prospects of new challenges in private practice.

In my last week at the U.S. Attorney's office, James and I finally had a long heart-to-heart conversation over coffee. It turned out that both of us were leaving the feds for private practice.

"You know, Diana, I'll be leaving the office later this year. After Reagan appoints a Republican U.S. Attorney replacement."

"Going back to your old firm?"

"Sure. And a less structured professional life. Back to the antics of the Democrats, where I'll feel more freedom with my favorite political issues."

"Sounds like a good thing."

"Yeah, on my own, no one from D.C. breathing down my neck."

I smiled and understood his relief. He was an avid political animal, marching to his own drummer.

"So, Diana, you're going to join those three-piece suit guys in private practice?"

"Well, yes, I guess you could say that. They have exactly the trial practice I want to be a part of."

I didn't want to mention my hope to improve my personal life.

"Actually, I know a couple of the lawyers there. Who have the right political stuff."

He meant left-leaning Democrats. After I joined the private firm, I would discover this first-hand.

Then James and I chatted amiably about the immigration case still going on, now managed almost entirely by the INS lawyers in D.C.

"You'll probably be relieved to get away from the two class action cases, right?" James continued.

"Well, yes. So much thorny bullshit by the INS in the immigration case. It adds to the challenge of defending. And who knows what will eventually come out in the DOE sex discrimination litigation."

"You got that right about the INS bullshit."

He didn't want to get into the details, but understood my concerns, I felt sure. I changed the subject.

"There's a new wave of women lawyers coming

along." I paused while he switched gears.

"With the bright interns you hired, it's a promising atmosphere here for women," I said.

"I hope so."

"James, the women interns followed me around like chicks with a mother hen. Having them in the office means a lot to me."

I felt a little teary-eyed.

"Time to get back to the office. Let's go," James said, as he got up from the table. I knew he wanted to leave before things got too sentimental. He didn't go for that.

When I left the USA's office, James gave me a bottle of fine wine from his basement cache, with a taped-on personal note: "Nothing I like better than old wine and old broads." By 1981, I was into my 40s. When I read his note, it choked me up, but he'd already left my going-away party in his enigmatic way. He had a habit of disappearing without a visible stir, often in the background.

I knew James was a solid fan of mine, although he never actually said so. I owed a lot to him.

Chapter 19

Psycho Sam

ENTERING PRIVATE PRACTICE WAS A WORLD APART from my first-day encounter as a federal prosecutor with the weird flag salute initiation or stunt. Instead, flowers appeared on my desk in my new office, along with jovial welcomes from lawyers and staff. I felt privileged to join an established law firm noted for its quality lawyers' expertise in all sorts of civil litigation, including business, real estate, tax, estates and insurance cases for corporate and individual clients.

Each of the firm's lawyers spent one-on-one time with me, briefing me about their specialties, client base and history with the firm. They surrounded me with get-acquainted talk that was friendly and comfortable. A couple of the older partners, obviously curious, put effort into their best behavior for a woman lawyer entering their all-male bastion. I relaxed and leaned into the welcome, ready to start my actual lawyering.

For weeks, I reviewed pending litigation files and did basic research, similar to the intern work I did as a law student. It was an opportunity to learn about typical clients and their connections with the firm, as well as handle actual files of meaty civil litigation going on. I dug in, eager to show my stuff, meet clients and make my way into their confidence.

Gary, the senior partner, assigned me to work on files for a firm client who had multiple legal matters pending. I began by doing research and legal opinion memos for Sam Ruben, a short, heavy set, dark-haired man with graying sideburns, beady eyes and an impatient way of speaking that came across as orders. Always in motion with this deal or that, Sam was not easy to please. I usually found myself re-working my legal opinions after his review. Rather than hear about pros and cons of an issue, he demanded aggressive plans for winning a lawsuit and coming out on top in a disputed deal.

My first solo case for Sam involved a business contract, which began innocently enough.

Sam was a longtime client, a small businessman who owned a jewelry shop on the floor below our law firm in a vintage brick building in the heart of downtown Spokane. He had a low-stakes dispute about the lease for his shop which had developed into a lawsuit in the limited jurisdiction district court, a division of the state court system. Gary, the senior partner, thought it would be a good start for me.

At first Sam was reluctant to have me work the case for him. Asked a lot of questions about my federal practice, cases that went to trial and whether I won or not. Did I know the ins and outs of leases and specific contract clauses? With every conversation, Sam required explanations about strategy and how would I crush the opposing party. I tried my best to act like a bulldog with him, so Sam gradually came around and warmed up to me. He wanted litigation with a bring-it-on attitude. One of those "wannabe lawyer" types who knows everything and wants to run the lawsuit.

Gary was a seasoned business litigation lawyer in his 60's, with serious intensity and soft-spoken authority, who kept his eye on my first case for Sam because I was the firm newbie. Despite Sam's constant interference, I prepared the trial brief, motions and managed the procedural issues which were my strengths. The Civil Rules of Procedure in state court are virtually the same as in federal court, so I had a history of using these rules to advantage. Gary convinced Sam that I could try the case myself, which pleased me.

In the non-jury trial of the case, the judge ruled in our favor. Sam became ecstatic when I successfully argued for payment of attorneys' fees from the losing party, because of an obscure contract clause. Sam hadn't realized the clause allowed an award of actual attorneys' fees as the prevailing party. This meant that Sam's legal fees had to be paid by his opponent. This part made him think I was a star.

Sam continued to come up with crazy unworkable schemes that would never win lawsuits. He was volatile, unpredictable and intent on being in control. I was challenged to get him to listen and understand why his ideas wouldn't work. Sam required constant restraint of his oppressive approaches to business dealings which often spelled trouble.

He owned industrial property and other investments in addition to his jewelry shop, always in need of legal advice. Sam frequently threatened lawsuits if things didn't go his way. His opponents on the other side of contentious dealings responded with more of the same. His antagonists would describe Sam as litigious. I played the role of feisty and fearless. Sam began to settle in, now calling me *his* lawyer.

Sam showed up regularly with legal questions, new disputes or lawsuits, so he became a familiar figure. Sometimes we would work over lunch or coffee out of the office. He preferred going out.

When he got into a messy legal hassle with his next-door neighbor over a property line disagreement about a portion of their common driveway, the relationship heated up into a physical confrontation with his neighbor. Sam and the neighbor ended up pushing, shoving, name calling and a couple of punches. The neighbor sued for damages for assault as well as a redrawing of the property line, a legal concept of "adverse possession."

The neighbor had been using part of the gravel driveway for over a decade. Sam decided to cut off the neighbor's use by blocking the driveway. I never got the real reason from Sam, as his motivation seemed to be that his neighbor was "a worthless asshole." The neighbor was furious, had a survey done, hired a lawyer, and sued Sam to acquire the disputed property on the basis of continued usage.

When Sam arrived at my office with the Summons and Complaint, he barked out, "This is war." He slapped the legal papers on my desk. I took a deep breath.

"Just let me read through this, Sam. Calm down and have some coffee while you're waiting."

"No, dammit, get this thing going."

He sat there fidgeting while I read though the documents and attachments, making a few notes.

He finally jumped up. "Let's go to lunch."

"Hold on, I need to get the Notice of Appearance started first." I buzzed for my secretary.

Then Sam and I headed out for lunch together, which was becoming a time-consuming routine. Not that he didn't pay for my time while we were "at lunch," which usually turned out to be much more than the legal advice was worth. Especially since he insisted on drinking a martini before lunch was served. Sometimes I had a martini too, just to show him I was a tough broad and could knock one down. He liked that.

Once Sam's property case was set for trial, the plaintiff/neighbor had a mild heart attack, so the trial date was postponed. While that case lingered on, Sam became antsy and impatient. But he had other deals to worry about.

Always needing legal opinions on his business dealings and potential litigation, he continued to show up at the office expecting me to see him, often without an appointment. Or he would call and want me to meet him somewhere, a popular lunch spot in town, or at the exclusive men's social club. Sometimes we went to a local bistro where he knew people.

I'd bring the files and my yellow legal pad in my briefcase, take some notes and give advice. Sometimes he wanted to talk about other things—his family, ex-wives, or business plans for all his great money-making ventures. The movers and shakers in town knew him. Sam would make sure they came over to our table to meet me—*his* lawyer. I felt uncomfortable, like a piece of jewelry on display from his shop. On the other hand, we were a ball-busting team by that point, and I was mostly enjoying it.

"Hey Diana, one of these days I'll take you out to the motel I'm thinking of buying, just to look it over and see what you think."

I blinked back my surprise and small spike of fear. Over my dead body, I thought. I'm not one to get intimidated easily. I rely on my confidence and bravado to get me through the bad stuff. And of course, the small pistol I keep under the seat in my car. Sam droned on as he drank his pre-lunch martini.

When we walked around town to and from lunch and coffee places, he'd wave his hands all over the place. He'd grab my arm to make a point. Or put his hand on my back or around my waist in a brief familiar way, like I was his girlfriend. I'd move away. Then he'd start in again. I felt like slapping him.

Sometimes I'd purposely carry my brief case between us to obstruct his grabby hands as we walked on the street. I didn't call him on it, because of the firm's longtime client relationship, and all the fees I brought in for Sam's cases. If I did confront him, I could imagine Sam complaining to Gary about me for some phony reason. Maybe get me fired. As a new associate, I felt trapped by this stealthy lecher, although at some level I was flying pretty high.

Sam's lawsuit defending the neighbor's assault and property claim finally had a trial date. Sam and I met several times to plan our strategy. Strategy was key with him, and he had to be in charge of it. I insisted we meet in my office where I could access the files.

On the day of trial, Sam and I arrived at the courthouse ready for anything. As we sat close together in the courtroom awaiting assignment to a trial courtroom, Sam nudged me.

"I'm ready," he whispered.

"Good."

His hand moved imperceptibly to his suit jacket and he opened his lapel slightly. I glanced over and saw the edge of a hefty hand gun in a shoulder holster. My eyes widened and my body tensed. Just then the judge announced our assigned courtroom. I pushed Sam to get up and we stumbled into the hallway. I was seething with anger, and shoved him down the hall where we could talk privately.

"What the hell are you doing with that gun?" I hissed.

"Just packing heat."

"You *can't* have a gun in here."

I tried to speak softly but almost shouted.

"Get it out of here."

"It's for protection."

"No guns allowed in the courthouse. Go put it in your car."

He balked and stood still for a few seconds.

"Now."

He left the courthouse and came back to find me sitting on a bench in the hallway thoroughly rattled. In those days, there was no security in state courthouses, even for judges. No scanners, no checkpoints. Firearms were not permitted, but the ban was not actively enforced that I ever noticed. Sam had simply walked in with his gun without detection.

What a way to start a trial. But we had to. Most of the trial is a blur to me now. Amazingly, I successfully defended the case, but felt no joy afterwards, only relief. Sam knew I was pissed off about the gun in the courtroom. He actually said he was sorry, then went on crowing about the courtroom win.

We celebrated with martinis and a lavish lunch at his club. Sam was relaxed in a strangely subdued appreciative mood.

"You're pretty good, Diana. I'm impressed."

"Thanks."

I think I'll have you handle my motel deal that's falling apart. I need good legal firepower, and maybe a lawsuit if things don't go right."

"Okay."

Walking back from our long lunch, he stopped and turned the corner into his parking lot.

"Come on, I have to get something from my car," he said.

When we got to the car, he opened the passenger side and said, "Get in."

I stopped, and said "Why?"

"I need to show you the bullshit at the motel, the things they're trying to put over on me in this deal. It's the driveway access and parking that's all screwed up. Not the way the drawings showed. They flat out lied to me."

I got in the car and he drove to the edge of town. The motel had been closed for renovation, but no one was around that I could see. Sam had some keys.

"Here, I'll show you the lobby and office first."

We walked around, went in the lobby as he talked about the great deal he was getting.

He unlocked a room next to the lobby and we looked in.

"Nice rooms, huh?"

Then he grabbed me, kissed me and pushed me over and down on the bed. He was stronger than I expected.

In the fog of my martini lunch, I was so stunned, I hardly resisted. As I began to push back, he was quick, flipped up my skirt, and groped my crotch while he pinned my arm. Then he was on top and I was caught.

"Hey, stop. Stop it," I yelled.

No one to hear.

I struggled, kicked and tried to hit him. His strong hands restrained my arms. I was pinned down, yelling and kicking. We finally rolled off the bed together and hit the floor. He let go and gave up the fight. He was hopping mad. So was I.

I got up, ran into the bathroom and locked the door. My heart was racing. Shit, I was almost raped. Wet fear drenched my skin. I thought of the pistol back in my car in the city parking lot. A lot of good it did me there. I was trapped.

Sam apologized and apologized, shouting at the bathroom door.

"Diana, come on out. I'm sorry. I'm sorry. Don't know what I was thinking.

"I was kidding—just to see what you'd do," he added. I was scared to unlock the door.

"We'd be good together, you know."

I felt like vomiting.

I had no choice eventually but to come out. He could tell I was furious. He acted like nothing happened. We went back to his car, got in and he drove back to town.

On the way back, he said something about being drunk and just losing it. Yeah, right.

I told him to let me out on the street corner near my office. I didn't go in, but ran to my car and drove myself home in a daze to figure all this out. I felt guilty and confused. And mad as hell. I needed to report this fucking pervert.

Then I thought of all the risky downsides of reporting Sam. What about my job with the firm? What about all the consternation it would cause? Would I be blamed? Maybe I should actually keep this shit to myself and not say anything. But that seemed so wrong. I was in shock. Frustrated and mixed-up.

At home I went to bed and told Michael and the kids I felt sick from some food I ate. I just lay there in a weird fog, wondering if I was losing my mind. Kept going over what had happened, and what I could have done. I thought of my pistol tucked away under the seat of my car, but of course that would have been no help since we had been in Sam's car. I knew he kept his gun in his car.

I couldn't make sense of anything. Was it my fault, did I lead him on? I felt thoroughly embarrassed. How could I tell my partners? Or anybody? After all, I wasn't actually raped. Was it just an aggressive pass at me that went wrong?

In the end, I figured the only thing was to show up the office the next morning and act like everything was okay.

Then things with Sam went back to their usual pattern. He would call with some trivial legal question or emergency and want to meet for lunch. Although I hated to be around Sam after the motel attack, I felt obligated to continue at first, but no more martinis at lunch for me.

Meanwhile, senior partner Gary gave me kudos, comments like how well I was doing at the firm. Bringing in substantial fees and such. How Sam thought so highly of me, and "what a good lawyer I was."

Ever since I joined the firm, one of the junior partner guys made himself available to me, answering my many questions. A friendly go-to guy, Don had me work with him on trial support in a few cases. He was a crackerjack lawyer, with a reddish blond crewcut, boyish face, and a sense of humor, with a record of phenomenal successes in the courtroom. He filled me in on firm politics and client preferences. We got to know each other, having coffee now and then. I decided to tell Don about Sam's gun-in-the-courtroom incident. He was stunned.

"Why didn't you mention this before?" he said.

"I didn't want to rock the boat with one of Gary's regular clients, firm history, fees, all that."

"Diana, nobody in the firm really wants to work with Sam," said Don. He told me the firm's tax lawyers hated it when they had to deal with Sam's financial records.

"Sam's books cause ethical concerns because they are so convoluted. He's unmanageable, always on the edge of blowing up, argumentative, and won't follow directions. He's walked out of the firm before, saying he won't come back. Then we cringe when he does."

"The client from hell."

"Exactly, to say the least. Gary keeps him on because of a long history with the firm. He's a member of the Temple. A constant flow of fees."

I sat there, taking this in. I knew I could trust Don. I took a deep breath, and told him of my "hands-on" problems with Sam. But I did not confess anything to Don about the motel encounter which still freaked me out. My misplaced guilt or possible complicity made me too worried about myself and my future with the firm if I revealed the ugly details of Sam's sexual move on me.

"Don, I just can't work with Sam anymore. He creeps me out with those long lunches to show me off to his friends. Sam puts his hands on and around me which makes me want to retch. It's repulsive and demeaning. I always have to be on guard when he moves toward me. I'm uncomfortable and it's getting worse. But I am embarrassed and don't want to bring this stuff up with the firm."

"Oh shit, you're kidding me."

"No, I'm not kidding you. But that personal part is just between us. Promise me."

Don nodded. We sat not saying anything for a long time. Don slumped in his chair as I continued.

"The gun thing at court. The uncontrollable temper. Monopolizing my time with trivial stuff. I'm being used as a prop and feel compromised. I've had it with this badass creep in so many ways."

Finally, Don sat up straight.

"Okay, look. I'll tell Gary, lay it all out, the gun in the courtroom, the aggression, all that. The fear. Gary will agree. You'll see."

Gary listened when Don met with him about Sam. I don't know exactly what Don told Gary. But they both knew that Sam was off the rails in many ways. Gary agreed that the gun thing in the courtroom was totally unacceptable and beyond limits. Said he would talk with Sam and tell him I was being reassigned, needed on other cases. Gary himself would work with Sam, then assign another new associate, a male, to work with this out-of-bounds client. My guilt didn't disappear, but I felt a huge load of relief.

I worried that Gary would hold this whole controversy with Sam against me. But he never mentioned it, except once.

"Diana, this isn't the first over-the-edge incident with Sam. It's for the best. Forget it." Gary wanted me to move on. To more productive work, he said.

If only he knew all the gory details, I thought to myself.

When I saw Sam in the office after that, I avoided him whenever possible. I could feel the revulsion and fear rise in me just at the sight of him.

During the next tax season, Sam exploded in a rage at one of our tax lawyers, chewed out Gary and everyone in the firm, saying he would never set foot in the firm again. I worried part of the fault would land on me. But nothing happened, and gradually psycho Sam faded away from my conscious awareness.

After Sam walked away from the firm, I had to tell my friend Josie about Sam and what had happened to me. She had a lot to say.

"That fucking rapist, you put up with him way too long. He needed to be reported and locked up."

"I know."

"Carrying a gun into the court room—a recipe for disaster. Then the actual sexual assault—attempted rape—at the motel. Diana, how could you keep that to yourself? How could you still work with him?"

"Josie, I was a new associate, less than a year in. It happened gradually. I was under so much pressure to succeed in the firm as the first woman. I couldn't make myself go crying to the firm."

"But Diana, you shouldn't endure that crap. The criminal behavior. The guy tried to rape you."

"I know, I know. But I felt guilty, going along with all his preliminary antics. Like why did I agree to go the motel with him? Was it partly my fault? What was I thinking?"

"Diana, it wasn't your fault. You're over-analyzing this—the victim's reaction. Stop it. Stop it."

I sat there, feeling like a helpless little girl. I couldn't say anything, trying to breathe through my choked-up confusion. I started blubbering again.

"Well, yeah. It's ridiculous that I kept the motel thing to myself. He's a bully, a loser, dangerous. He should be locked up as a sexual predator. Period."

"A criminal, Diana."

We sat there at Parno's, sipping wine and silent, each with our own thoughts. Me seething all over again. Josie's comments made me remember my own strength, and how I should set boundaries sooner, not later. To speak up when needed, despite my personal fears. Recognize how it's often hard for something good to come from a bad beginning.

We were out of words and energy, and acted like that was the end of it. Still, I was totally frustrated. I hadn't even told Michael about Sam's attack on me. Maybe someday. I tried to check it off as a hazard of working with a predatory creep who thought he could treat me any way he wanted and get away with it. In the end, at least I had some support from my firm. Although they never got the entire story.

"Maybe I should start carrying my pistol in my purse more often. Shoot the next guy who tries something."

We sat there again in silence for a long time. I needed to acknowledge unexpected and dangerous situations that arose in this emotionally-charged, competitive world of litigation. And yet in most ways—I loved that world.

Josie and I moved on to gossip about our law school buddies. Humor as a frequent antidote to our frustrations. Working our way into the legal world meant barriers, and sometimes we had to kick the shit out of them, if only verbally to each other, to work off the anger.

We realized that we were taking on the male lawyers' establishment one small step at a time. Some lawyers and clients refused to see us as lawyers first. Not all were that way—there were plenty of good guys. But neither Josie nor I was blessed with abundant patience, even after being in practice for awhile. We made our way in measured steps, sometimes large and mostly small, as we tripped along in our high heels.

Chapter 20

Cultural Lesson

AN UNEXPECTED TELEPHONE CALL CAME TO ME from Randy, the local Immigration boss, someone I knew from my work in the U.S. Attorney's office. He had an asylum case, an immigrant from Iran who needed a lawyer. Right away.

Randy wanted to refer the Iranian woman to me because I had "experience with immigration law." That surprised me, as I knew little about general immigration law except for my one big case involving INS raids of the migrant workers' camps in eastern Washington. I'd been out of the federal government for a few years now, and hadn't thought about my adventures, or misadventures, with the INS, since going into private practice in the early '80s.

Randy had always been up front, helpful and understanding of the issues raised during the prolonged INS litigation. He would cut to the chase without bullshit about the shortcomings of some INS procedures, and was my go-to guy for clarification of the INS hierarchy in D.C. Now this urgent request for me to take an asylum case. Puzzling. I didn't get it.

"Randy, I know little about the particulars of immigration law. Nothing about asylum. I can't take this kind of case,"

"You're the only one I could think of to help her. The hearing date is next week. Leah is a former university student who overstayed her visa, like so many others. She's desperate and hopeless. Such a bright woman who would bring much to the U.S. as an immigrant, but for the asylum problem."

Why was Randy so persistent? I felt he was pressuring me. There must be other lawyers more qualified to help this woman. What is his real connection with her? He's raised my curiosity, but I needed to say no.

"Randy, I don't feel comfortable handling an asylum petition."

I could hear him sigh.

"Okay, but how about just talking with her?" Randy wasn't taking no for an answer.

"Well, maybe I could refer her to some other lawyer who knows immigration law."

"Any way you could help her, Diana. Just be sure to never mention my name in connection with Leah's case. I can't be involved in this. You can say she came through Legal Services or the bar association referral if it comes up." He paused, pushing me to agree.

What was Randy's insistent concern about her situation and secretive about his connection with her? It seemed more than a conflict of interest. Maybe something going on between them, I imagined. I remembered Randy as a single, handsome and articulate officer, serious about his work with a down-to-earth sense of humor.

Randy counted as one of the good guys in the INS, as agent-in-charge when I worked with him. I surmised he stayed with his INS job because of eventual retirement benefits and didn't want to rock the boat. I thought back to our field trip "running after rabbits" and how he made sure I saw only a limited part of the operations. Was he protecting me as a newbie AUSA? Randy had kept me away from the agents' drinking fest in the evening after the raid. I could see he didn't fit the mold of some overly aggressive, unfeeling or rough name-calling Border Patrol agents. Randy had the sensitive personality women would notice.

I had mixed feelings, but agreed to see the Iranian woman.

Leah arrived at my law firm for her appointment the next morning with a leather briefcase full of papers.

She was dressed to the nines—expensive high heels, a glowing blue satin blouse under a sleek beige suit with designer lines. Her beautiful smooth face of creamy mocha skin surrounded her expressive black eyes with eyelashes to die for. At 26, she spoke English fluently without an accent. Her first impression of outward confidence contrasted with obvious inner shyness, as she dropped her eyes after speaking.

Leah was an Iranian exchange student who had grossly over-stayed her lawful visa. She was petrified, shaking like a leaf as she told me the details of her story.

In the time she was away from Iran as an American foreign exchange student, the newly-installed Iranian government had terrorized her Catholic family.

Her sister had been intimidated and threatened for trivial violations of the dress codes. Her loving grandparents were arrested and sent away to some unknown location. The family couldn't practice their Catholicism, and secret gatherings for Mass would end badly if they were caught. Her brother's coerced army life was at a standstill because he couldn't pursue his college education.

Leah had American friends who encouraged her to stay in America. She had researched the statutes herself and managed to file a petition for asylum based on the grounds of her Catholicism as well as threats against her extended family. Leah was terrified to face the immigration service hearing without an attorney, she kept repeating.

"My Iranian Catholic family obtained a student visa for me as an exchange student. I began studies at Eastern Washington University. Now I am at Gonzaga, studying biology and health sciences." She showed me her documents, including her school papers and her expired student visa.

As she talked, I thought back to my connections and acquaintances at the INS because of my involvement defending the government's civil rights violations against immigrants. That case was all about INS illegal behavior and practices, nothing about asylum. During that time, I did make friends with some of the agents in INS and Border Patrol. I'd see Randy and others when I occasionally appeared at the federal courthouse in my private practice cases.

As Leah talked, I could feel her pain, drawn into her

fearful world by vivid descriptions of horrors at home, related in her low halting voice of despair.

"I'm panic-stricken to return to Iran. My family has much trouble."

She repeated worries about her grandparents' disappearance, and about how her brother was forced to join the army. Catholics could not go to church or Mass, because buildings had been destroyed. In between tears, she unfolded the dashed hopes and dreams of her sister's chance for higher education. And the worst—her fears about forcible return to Iran, crushing her own dreams.

"My friends here…some have asylum. Sometimes immigration people help with the papers. But one immigration man threatened me, to make me return home. He told me I'd never get asylum, to forget it and go back where I came from."

"What exactly will happen to you if you went back?"

"I don't know. I don't know. My father told me by telephone, you cannot come back Leah. It is bad, it is dangerous. He told me to stay here to be safe. He cried and said he loved me. That I was precious and we had no choice."

Leah sat in a crumpled mess in my office chair, her tears staining her satin blouse. Her shiny black hair fell over her face as she trembled and sobbed. My ambivalent resistance dissolved. I couldn't send her away.

She gave me her papers from the INS. I made copies. Her hearing date and possible deportation date loomed and she was desperate.

I told her to come back the next day while I researched her situation. I began working for her because I couldn't say no. I had fallen into the extreme distress of her abyss. Later that day I called the INS, filed a Notice of Appearance with a request for a continuance to delay Leah's deportation hearing.

I kept asking myself, why am I doing this? The asylum statutes were all new to me—confusing, ambiguous and vague. I needed help.

I called Alice, a long-ago passing acquaintance who was a clerk at the INS office. She gave me some leads, and I was grateful for her general directions about asylum.

"Foreign students frequently overstay their visas. The ones from Iran are complicated because of the tremendous turmoil with the regime change. Catholics in Iran are under siege," she said.

"Are the administrative courts granting asylum these days to Iranians?"

"In some cases, yes. It depends. You need to get the specifics from your client to see whether the situation fits. That's about all I can say."

I wanted more, but that was all she could give.

"Thanks so much, Alice."

"Good luck, Diana."

The statutes and the legislative guidelines for asylum were vague. My inexperience needled at me when I took a breath and realized the seriousness of what I was trying to do. Then I'd dig in again.

I had to find out more from Leah. She came in with details of persecution and escalating violence toward her family. The breaking into the family home, destruction of all religious icons, edicts forbidding all Catholic religious practices. The multiple cruelties to her brother involving his forcible army service, her sister as a virtual prisoner in her Catholic family home. I couldn't use all of it, as portions of her worries revealed much that would be counterproductive—cultural issues like clothing and activity restrictions on all Iranian women. Obviously, Leah had become quite aware of women's individual freedoms in America.

In preparing Leah's case, I wove the story of Leah's personal history in Iran and the U.S., especially Leah's educational accomplishments, her multiple language abilities, as well as Leah's serious intention to pursue post-graduate studies in a U.S. medical school.

In the end, I pieced together a persuasive narrative describing Leah's tragic conflicted situation, attached credible evidence for asylum together with Leah's supplemental affidavit and filed the papers at the immigration office. And crossed my fingers for good luck which was needed most.

As the hearing date approached, uneasiness and worry surrounded me, especially because of my inexperience as an immigration lawyer. This was a risky scenario for Leah. If I failed, she would be deported, her life permanently changed in horrible ways. Was I being presumptuous in my attempts to help her? My contrived confidence pushed me as if I knew what I was doing.

She appeared early at my office the day of the immigration hearing wearing an expensive silk print summer dress with a matching lavender beaded necklace and bracelet. Her anxious dark eyes and trembling hands gave away her emotions. She sat quiet and still in a corner of my office while I gathered folders into my briefcase, squared my shoulders and stood up.

"All ready?"

"I think so." That was all she could manage. I quietly echoed her thought to myself.

We walked together a few blocks to the federal courthouse on that summer day, our summer-strap high heels clicking against the sidewalk. Leah was tall like me, so we walked in step. Silence weighed me down. She was enveloped in an aura of fear.

Click, click. Click, click.

At the hearing, Leah was sworn in under oath. The INS presiding officer sat at his desk, taking in Leah's beauty, then glanced briefly over at me. I introduced her and made a few remarks. The small hearing room was less intimidating than a huge courtroom, but Leah probably didn't notice. By her side, I willed Leah to tell her story well.

She was articulate, believable and convincing, as the immigration officer listened intently. He may have been entranced by her lovely face and stunning appearance, her mannerisms and language, I don't know. But his focus on Leah told me he was listening. He asked a few clarifying questions, but made no comments that gave a clue what he was thinking. I made a few closing comments. After the 30-minute hearing he dismissed us to wait in the anteroom.

Leah and I sat in the straight government-issue chairs in the nondescript enclosed room with no windows, awaiting her fate. She cried softly, and dabbed her tears with a white lace-edged handkerchief. I wanted to hold her hand to reassure her, but that seemed inappropriate. She had private grief running through her body and mind. I could only be there, witness her pain, and pray that the immigration office would show mercy.

An hour went by. Others came and went as they were called into the inner hearing rooms of the immigration service. Finally, a young woman receptionist called Leah's name and escorted us back to the hearing room, where the officer sat behind his large imposing desk. He was looking down and shuffling papers. I could feel Leah holding her breath.

The officer looked up, turned on the recording device, and announced the name of the case. He recited the various assertions of Leah including the statements under oath in her affidavit, then paused. I felt myself choking, like I might have a coughing fit. He then looked at Leah directly, taking her in.

"Having considered all of the documents, information and evidence provided by petitioner, the applicant is hereby granted asylum in the United States, by the authority vested in me as a Hearing Officer of the Immigration and Naturalization Service, subject to the conditions enumerated herein."

He paused to take a breath, still expressionless, then set forth several requirements for reporting together with multiple forms to be completed. I let out my breath and replied. "Thank you."

Leah followed my lead and whispered, "Thank you." Tears welled up.

The officer handed me the Order and other documents, which I slipped into my brief case. Leah and I walked slowly out of the room, down the hall, into the elevator.

As the elevator descended, I put my briefcase down and rested my arm lightly around her shoulders. My face brushed hers, feeling the wet tears still on her cheeks. I could feel her shivering, not in fear but relief as she stood there alone in her thoughts. The elevator doors opened. Leah and I walked down the courthouse pavilion steps, and along the sidewalk in the glorious summer sunshine. No words needed.

Click, click. Click, click.

Up the stairs to my office reception area and into my office. Leah's face still glowed with her tears. I closed my office door and turned to her.

Leah dropped to the floor and knelt down. She began kissing my feet through the straps of my high heels. I stood there still as a statue, unable to move. I was shocked, uncomfortable and embarrassed. I wanted to lift her off the floor. I didn't know what to do. Why was she kissing my feet? I gently took her shoulders and pulled her up from the floor.

She threw her arms around me and whispered, "You saved my life. You saved my life."

We held each other for what seemed like an eternity. We breathed together until she gradually stopped sobbing.

Then she slowly began to laugh. We both laughed.

Until we were totally spent.

"What is next?" Leah finally asked.

"Come back to my secretary tomorrow for copies of the Order and the other papers. You will find all the instructions, and you can call if you have any questions."

I rested my hand lightly on her shoulder before she left, and closed my office door and sat at my desk in a fog. What had just happened? Had this been a cultural offering of ultimate thanks? I did not understand what she had done, but clearly felt her grateful spirit within me.

That was the last I saw of Leah. Nothing before or since ever compared to my experience with Leah, her true-life tales of family fear, cruelty, danger and life threats. Especially her expression of gratitude when she kissed my feet. I would not forget her.

As for the vaguely familiar INS officer who presided at Leah's hearing, I wasn't sure whether he knew anything about me, my past history in the U.S. Attorney's office or involvement with the INS class action case. Somehow in my imagination, I hoped my background may have been a possible unacknowledged factor in Leah's case decision.

This confusion about past connections swam around only once in a dream I had about Leah and Randy's possible liaison. Randy remained a mystery to me. But as an attorney, it wasn't my style to waste time speculating about that. I never heard back frrom Randy.

Chapter 21

Discrimination Hades

When I first met Darlene Renner, I couldn't help but admire her—a serious articulate woman in her late 50s, successful in the field of high-stakes finance. She was dressed for success in an expensive navy wool business suit, with a competent air about her. I could see myself listening to her investment advice and buying into her stock and bond portfolios in the Investment Department at the community's largest local bank.

After our conversation about generalities and her professional expertise, she fell apart. She could not contain incoherent emotional outbursts when she talked about what had happened. She crumpled up like the tissue in her shaking hand.

A long-time bank employee, Darlene began as a teller, then worked her way up to the current position as a successful bond trader in the Investment Department. Financially, she was pulling down a fantastic income consisting of salary plus commissions. Cash piled up for retirement like an overflowing treasure chest. Life was good for her and husband Hank.

Her alma mater was the school of hard knocks. Darlene began 25 years ago as a teller trainee. She was comfortable with numbers, quick in-her-head math. Reliability and accuracy were her marks. Her clear blue eyes, straight nose and high cheekbones gave her a classic look. Except when she drifted off into painful spaces during that first interview.

As a part-time teller, Darlene's bank customers were attracted to her polite manner and eager-to-please ways. They trusted her cheery smile and efficiency which helped her make friends with customers. Remembering people's names came easy to her. The bank valued her customer goodwill. She became a full-time bank employee when her children advanced to high school. That's when Darlene's career at the bank took off. She rose to head teller, then was promoted to higher administrative levels. As the bank grew, Darlene's responsibilities expanded.

When the bank first offered an investment program for their customers, Darlene applied for a place in the Investment Department, an entirely different type of financial job for her. The bank president encouraged her to apply, recognizing her skill and rapport with bank customers. Her personality fit well with the necessary marketing component of the new investment program. Darlene enrolled in banking and investment classes and passed the exam for securities licensing. Changes in banking regulations made this investment program possible, and banks were eager to jump into these lucrative opportunities in the 1980s.

Being the only woman in the department caused Darlene no concern, as everyone at the bank knew her well. Other bank employees had taken the investment classes and securities exam with her. Many of Darlene's customers from her teller days followed her for advice on their investments, so she developed a large book of customers who were friends.

The big reward in her new job was a generous commission schedule. Her base salary formed a small part of total compensation. Darlene's monthly paycheck ballooned with commissions, as her relationships with customers blossomed with successful investment returns.

In the meantime, Darlene's kids had grown up, and her husband Hank had just recovered from heart surgery which left him unable to continue his construction business. He accepted a job as a drafter in a small firm at a significant cut in pay. Darlene's fat paychecks buoyed them up, as she became the main support for the family.

The bank's Investment Department grew by adding experienced people from outside the bank. The bank raked in incredible income, and every broker benefitted from the market conditions. The commission rate schedule remained the same while the dollar sales volume grew. The Investment Department's employees' commissions kept rising, more than the bank had ever expected.

Most of the new hires in the Department came from brokerage houses with sophisticated expertise exceeding that of bank employees who had worked their way up. These outside brokers shared their expertise and complex shortcuts for handling transactions. The Investment Department buzzed like a beehive of activity, producing a financial honey pot.

Darlene worked as a noticeable minority of one woman in the sales group of aggressive outgoing younger guys. She liked the challenge and high-stakes atmosphere. At some point, she began to notice that she missed out on the new guys' impromptu casual meetings, inside jokes, and after-work activities where they discussed department business. None of this affected her financially, however, as she had a full active book of customers.

Until the bank reorganized the department into sections, and an outside hire named Richard became her boss. That's when the trouble started. He was a go-go trader in his early 40s who began by telling Darlene he expected her to be totally conversant with all the most complicated investment methods. Richard emphasized bond swaps and other high-level bond trading techniques that were his specialty.

Darlene's voice wavered as she described what happened next.

"Richard told me to study the manuals from his former brokerage firm experience. He expected me to know all this new complicated stuff to serve my customers. He kept repeating that investment trading is changing constantly, and I needed to keep up.

"I agreed to study up and understand everything he suggested—of course I would do that.

"He told me the high amount of my commissions required that I understand all—underline all— the complexities. He put down my entire background as a banking employee, and said the investment department is much different—a much higher level of expertise needed.

"So, I said okay, I'll start today.

"He wanted weekly reports on my progress." She flinched, telling about Richard's bossy instructions.

Darlene busied herself with further study. As time went by, she noticed that a couple of her old clients moved accounts over to buddies of her boss. When she brought this up to him, he told her that the guys handled some transactions while she was tied up studying. That meant they got the commissions from the individual transactions.

She began to realize that she received very few new clients, even though the ordinary procedure was to rotate assignment of new clients where there was no prior relationship. She felt the shadow of Richard's watchfulness, keeping close track of her transactions and commissions.

"Then I told Richard about errors when other traders got commissions from client transactions I handled, even though I felt hesitant to call the traders out. Their aggressive cutthroat tactics intimidated me. Richard never helped me correct the errors."

She paused to breathe through her shaking voice. I got her a glass of water.

"Take your time, Darlene. What happened after that?"

"In my first performance review by Richard, I received *five* critical comments. I was puzzled and afraid. And scared because I'd never been treated like this before at the bank. I was unable to respond or contradict his comments, and my only option was to try harder.

"I began to seriously doubt myself. I could feel

more hot flashes and less self-confidence. My nervous uncertainty affected my performance."

She made an appointment with her doctor about her anxiety and sleepless nights. He prescribed an antidepressant.

Darlene gradually disappeared into a fog as she told her story, and didn't seem to realize that Hank and I were in the room. All of a sudden, she stood up and looked around as if lost. I took her hand and helped her sit back down.

"Darlene, Darlene. Now tell me more about what happened after you saw your doctor. Did that help?"

She swallowed, suppressed a sob, looked up, and began again.

"No. Richard, the boss, he made me feel stupid and incompetent. I was losing ground. I couldn't do my job under a microscope. All by myself.

"Those guys in the office told back-slapping jokes after the markets closed for the day. If I tried to join in, I was ignored and the atmosphere got quiet. If I didn't pay attention to them, I felt isolated."

She shifted in her chair, and repeated, "Those guys, those guys…."

"Those guys grabbed my best customers. I didn't know how to stop them. Richard avoided me for weeks, and then hit me with an interim performance review. I'd never even heard of an interim review. He just dropped the review folder on my desk. No meeting, conversation, or chance to ask questions or get feedback. The review said my performance was unsatisfactory—*unsatisfactory*—in job knowledge, attitude, cooperation, and of all things, development of new business.

"I was obsessed that Richard and his guys were forcing me out."

"Darlene, take your time. Tell me what you did then."

"I…I…I guess…panicked, thinking—will I be fired?"

During that time, Darlene wasn't included in planning sessions. Office memos, reports and routine department paperwork never came to her.

"Was I scratched from the distribution list and failed to notice? I couldn't keep track of *anything*," she wailed, as Hank reached over and took her hand.

"Darlene, take a moment. Just breathe as best you can and then tell us the rest." We sat there for a few minutes that seemed like an hour as she tried to compose herself.

"Okay, okay, I finally got my courage up to talk with Richard, asked what this interim review was based on, what it meant. Told him I'd been a bank employee for 25 years, and never seen anything like this. What was going on?

"He wouldn't give me details, no specifics. Just…I wasn't keeping up. I was stunned, speechless. Felt like I'd been slapped hard in the face.

"Richard just sat there looking at me until I lost control and couldn't feel anything. He said something about my longevity at the bank, said I'd had a good run. To think about *retirement*.

"Then he says, what about my husband's health problems? Don't I need to be home with him now?"

She couldn't hold the tears back. I told her to slow

down, just try to relax.

"He, he, said that maybe that would be the best thing for me. To retire. Retire?

"I just blanked out and dragged myself from Richard's office, grabbed my purse, and got out of there."

She never returned to the bank.

I stopped the interview with her, as she was completely spent. Guided her and Hank out of the office, saying we'd continue the next day.

Next day's office meeting brought a paralyzed Darlene, holding tightly to her husband's arm. Hank, a slightly balding man, with thick glasses and a permanent frown, did most of the talking. Darlene sat there silently, adding details, only a word or two, now and then, as if in a catatonic state.

One thing was certain, she would "never set foot in the bank again."

"Don't make me go back there," Darlene repeated, looking directly at Hank, as if she just remembered he was sitting next to her.

After her fateful last day at the bank, Darlene was referred by her physician to a psychologist for counseling, along with continuation of the anti-depressants.

The following week when I saw the Renners again, Darlene showed up with angry energy and rational responses to my questions. I explained the relevant laws against sexual harassment, wrongful termination and hostile work environment, and my plan to do extensive research.

It turned out that her boss had likely committed unfair employment practices which could trigger the bank's liability, creating a hostile work environment and possible wrongful termination. Darlene's new boss and traders in the Investment Department obviously shoved her out of their realm because she didn't fit in—her age and gender most notably. She raked in top commissions which irritated them. No one helped her or stood up for her. Darlene didn't know what the new rules were or how to fight back. Whatever she attempted seemed to backfire. Richard's intimidation virtually ordered her out of the bank, even though he didn't actually say, "You're fired."

I agreed to accept the case on a contingency basis, knowing full well that this would not be an easy ride. Yet it seemed that the inherent unfairness based upon Darlene's sex and age would jump out at a jury. Of course, that alone would not fulfill all the legal requirements.

In the 1980s, the state of actionable discrimination law included "hostile environment in terms and conditions of employment" which could create liability. In addition, the wrongful termination would have to be construed as a "constructive discharge" claim since Darlene's boss did not actually "pink slip" her. An implied termination depends upon all the circumstances, "whether a reasonable person in Darlene's situation would conclude she had been fired."

The bank would respond that Darlene had quit, just walked out of the office one day and refused to return. They would contend that Darlene should have pursued other options with bank officials or the personnel department to have her concerns heard. They would argue mightily the lack of credible proof and "no documentation."

During pretrial discovery, the bank subpoenaed Darlene's medical records, which added to her humiliation. Bank officials, even her former friends and colleagues, were reluctant to give any helpful testimony, at least on the record. They still worked for the bank and wanted to remain there—self-interest prevailed.

At her deposition, Darlene shook with nervous twitches. Intimidation hung heavy over her and husband Hank, while Richard and another bank representative glared at them across the table. Representatives of the bank were allowed in the deposition room according to the rules of civil procedure in pretrial discovery. Darlene avoided Richard's steely stare during her deposition, but gave remarkably descriptive testimony once she got angry and fought for herself.

A junior associate and I spent endless hours, weeks and months preparing the case for trial. We researched and wrote briefs on every possible issue, and drafted advance motions in limine to exclude irrelevant evidence. Our time-consuming preparation of witness testimony were dress rehearsals for trial. Darlene needed a lot of encouragement to overcome her ever-present fear and anxiety.

I fought similar feelings but could show only confidence and optimism. By this time, Darlene and I were locked together in combat with the bank, and the battle became personal for me. My closeness with the plaintiff required extra effort to disguise my feelings, even though my lawyer's role required objectivity.

After substantial pretrial discovery, my request for settlement negotiation talks went nowhere with the bank.

Civil cases have two issues: liability and damages. As for liability, the "he said—she said" part together with the difficulty of proving a hostile work environment was a tough reach. Darlene didn't exude the suave, likeable confidence of her young brash boss. Credibility of the parties and witnesses was key when a case unfolded before a jury. The jury must be educated about the insidious, often hidden particulars involving discriminatory intent and actions. They must agree to follow the judge's written instructions on liability.

The damages issue was easier to prove, assuming liability was established. Because Darlene earned large commissions in addition to salary, her lost income claim was huge. We had projected out ten years to her planned retirement. Our exhibit boards showed damages in the millions. We hoped the jury didn't flinch because of the high dollars involved.

If the bank lost the case, the monetary award would be enormous, not to mention the bad press, and potential loss of prestige for the old established community bank. As far as newspaper coverage during the lengthy trial, a local reporter sat in the courtroom off and on, but not a single news article ever appeared. I later wondered, was there some friendly connection or agreement between the bank and the newspaper to hold back press coverage?

One of our senior partners worked with me in the three-week trial, handling the medical testimony.

Bert was an experienced "trial horse" with silver hair, sincere blue eyes and an easygoing way of moving around the courtroom in an unhurried familiar way. His persuasive success with juries over decades was well-recognized. An extra benefit would be the balance of an older male presence on our litigation team in an attempt to override the inherent feminine vs. masculine energy on the face of our struggle. Bert deftly presented the professional medical testimony for the purpose of showing Darlene's significant emotional distress damages.

The medical witnesses described how Darlene's need for medical treatment and psychological counseling resulted directly from the bank's treatment of her, with particular emphasis on the last interview Darlene had with Richard when he basically told her to move on and retire. Which in final argument, I characterized as the "put up with it—or get out" dilemma in which Darlene was trapped.

The bank hotly contested every issue with their slick out-of-town legal defense team. Their devious methods and marginal cooperation had shown itself in pretrial discovery and scheduling. In the courtroom, these defense lawyers exuded an overly polite attitude toward my client and me. Being so thoroughly immersed in the case, Darlene and I probably looked like best friends to the jurors, as "Mrs. Renner, plaintiff" and "Mrs. Keatts, her lawyer." In our long ordeal of fighting with the obstreperous bank officials and their lawyers, she and I had bonded as I fought with passion for her in and out the courtroom. Outside of the jury's presence, I had to request the judge to stop the defense from calling me Mrs. and use the address "Ms." or "Counsel" in the courtroom, as my marital status was irrelevant. Good grief, I thought we were past that.

I'd go home and give Michael a disjointed briefing each day after court.

"I'm feeling Darlene's pain. Like we are one presence, one force."

"That sounds weird. You're supposed to be her lawyer after all."

"I know. Maybe too intense. Sometimes I have these wild thoughts—am I becoming Darlene?"

"Diana, come on, you need to calm down."

"I feel sometimes I'm losing it because I want to win this case so badly."

"You said it would be tough, with the unsettled law. People not understanding what hostile environment and all that other stuff means."

"I know. We have so much time and money invested. Not to mention the emotional part."

He hugged me, and we went on to other things, like our grandson and his new antics. This was what I needed, a grounding, to be able to go on. The daily battles were eating me up, and I was feeling this oddball fear, edges roughing me up most of the time. Michael and I had a quiet dinner, then I disappeared into our study to prepare for the next day at trial.

On the last day of trial after the case was sent to the jury, I felt relief mixed with trepidation. Our trial team was exhausted, and yet needed to show upbeat energy for our clients. Bert and I and the sharp new associate who had done a bang-up job on trial support, gathered at our office with Darlene and Hank. They wanted to rehash parts of the trial and had many "what-if " questions. We told them not to expect a verdict that late in the day. Now it was the jury's turn to work.

I fretted into the night. Prayed a little.

The next afternoon the jury came in with a verdict for the defense. It felt like a tornado hit me in the gut. Darlene burst into tears, and Hank blanched, putting his arm around her. My partner and I had to wear our expressionless masks as we asked for polling of the jury, in which each juror had to state whether it was his or her "verdict and the verdict of the jury." They all responded "yes."

We guided the clients out of the courtroom, into the courthouse conference room. We tried to make sense of the verdict for them. Darlene and I both had tears. We commiserated until the courthouse clerk told us they needed to lock up for the day. We were all shell-shocked, emotions drained and distress covering us like a shroud.

I was left with the image of Hank's arm around Darlene's shoulders as they limped away together.

Michael found me lying on the bed in my courtroom clothes when he came home from work. I blubbered about the verdict, tears and sobs getting in the way. My thoughts were jumbled, trying to dredge up a basis for appeal, but couldn't think straight. That night I spent hours re-hashing the trial until daylight, my body weighing a ton. I don't remember sleeping.

I had to face my law firm, the partners, other lawyers

and our energetic staff who worked on this important case. I dreaded making an appearance. Failure washed over me. I finally showed up, and spent the entire day in the office explaining, going over the issues, re-thinking the trial strategy, second-guessing everything.

I reeled with feelings of guilt and failure. I knew that sometimes you win, sometimes you lose in court, but I hadn't actually lost many cases in my career. This big loss threw me. The impact of the trial expenses, and overwhelming consumption of the firm's resources bit into my pride. Most of the deposition, witness and subpoena costs had to be paid by Darlene and Hank. But all the hours, weeks, and months of work and costly preparation by me and others, together with the investment that the firm made upon my recommendation ended up for naught.

If we had won, the firm's percentage of the verdict as well as our actual costs and attorney's fees award provided by statute, would have been substantial. The stunning defense verdict was not only a huge financial loss but much more. Defeat followed me around like a painful shadow I couldn't shake.

We analyzed the case for appeal and concluded that the issues could not sustain a successful run. I met with Darlene and Hank to explain the law and reasons for our recommendation of no appeal. I spent time helping Darlene understand what had happened, while I myself didn't. I kept thinking, where did I screw up? Dark clouds flew in and out. I wanted clarity and none came.

On the other hand, after the initial verdict and a meeting or two with Darlene and Hank, I noticed that she had recovered noticeable confidence, which I did not expect. Darlene even said she understood the jury's verdict, voicing stoicism about the result. She acted almost satisfied with her day in court. After baring her soul in front of the jury about her mistreatment and suffering, she showed surprising recovery. At one of our meetings, she put her arm around me in a comforting way.

"It's okay, it will be okay, Diana," she said.

Darlene got to tell her story. It wasn't really about the money.

She and Hank paid the firm reimbursement of $30,000 for the discovery costs and expenses of trial, as they were ethically required to do. Then they took off for a motor home trip to California. When Darlene described their travel plans, she pictured their trip as "a celebration of getting their life back." They would drive away from the enormous strain of the ordeal.

As for me, I could not get it back together. I obsessively re-thought the case. Re-analyzed depositions and trial testimony, relived court conferences, jury selection and instructions. Held on to my zeal for the case. Not very healthy, I thought. But I couldn't let go.

When my friend Josie and I finally got together after the trial, I could bare my soul to her.

"Why didn't the jury get it? Did the jurors dislike Darlene? And me? How did I screw up?"

On and on I went, as she listened.

"Did I get too close to my client? Put too much of myself in the case?"

"No, no and no. Listen to me, Diana, pull yourself together. Remember, this case was brought at a time when hostile environment and discrimination laws are still emerging. The public isn't tuned in to understand the nuances of discrimination. Don't blame yourself."

"But it seemed so obvious that the young males came into the bank, and shoved Darlene under the bus for all the wrong reasons. Illegal reasons. Then her asshole boss wanted her out as soon as he had the authority. Seems so clear to me."

"Diana, think about this. She was a middle-aged woman, came up from a part-time teller, to making more money than the rest of them because she had the bank's customers from her past. They resented her. She wasn't one of them. Getting rid of her was prime so they could make more money without her. They were wily liars without a smoking gun file. Uphill battle."

"Yeah, but why couldn't the jurors see that?"

Josie shrugged and continued.

"The jurors saw all that money she was making. Way more than the jurors have ever seen. Claiming ten years' worth of lost wages until normal retirement. Emotional distress damages. The jurors could be thinking, how much money does she want? She's already made a bundle."

"Yeah, but the jurors have to follow the law and the jury instructions the judge gave them."

"Diana, we both know that issues of fact dominate liability issues. You had no transcripts of conversations, only the performance reviews. Darlene's credibility as to what was said, was on the line. They didn't go with her version."

"Yeah, I know...."

We sat there with our own thoughts. In some ways, it was easier hearing this from Josie. I trusted her.

"You know, Diana, this cruel hell of discrimination takes so many forms. Think about yourself and what you've gone through. I've told you about some of my crap. Your client Darlene's reaction was to run and hide. She didn't know how to fight those jerks inside the bank. She fought it only when you gave her a chance. Sounds like the most important part to her was getting her story out."

"Well, I guess. But I cringe about the way she was treated. It was so wrong. Things have to change more than a little."

"Of course, of course. Absolutely."

We were spent with our conversation. We both shuffled around in our chairs. I had listened to her and let it sink in. I suppose I needed Josie's pragmatic advice, something to bring me back to reality and my future. I took a deep breath and changed the subject.

"So, on a more positive note, how are things with your practice?"

"Well, let me tell you about this incredible criminal case I tried just last week...."

We talked until late, and I needed to get home. I couldn't shake off all the echoing jitters I felt about Darlene's case. The next day, I busied myself with clients needing attention. But I still felt the sting of the big discrimination case, letting down a bunch of people and feeling like a miserable failure.

At home, I was cranky, pre-occupied and short-tempered. I had a hard time feeling settled and grounded. Michael was sick and tired of my obsession.

"Diana, get a grip. There are worse things than losing a case. Move on, that's what healing is about."

"Oh yeah, I know, everybody says that. But I just can't move on."

I could feel myself giving in to tears. Michael came over and pulled me to him.

"Okay, look. How about this. Why don't we go over to Seattle on Friday, take a weekend off?"

We did, and it helped. I had plenty of work to do, and making partner was one of them. I needed to get back on track, increase my billable hours and re-connect with my colleagues in the firm in a positive way.

I forced myself to dig into my backlog of civil cases, racking up successful results for clients and respectable billable hour totals. I also worked with our office manager and a partner to prepare for our firm retreat, an annual two-day event of bonding and camaraderie that I was looking forward to.

The event was held at a nearby lake resort, where we had meetings about firm business and future planning. I thrived in the atmosphere of feeling part of a close-knit professional group who wanted the same things I did. I came home feeling grateful to be in with this smart, high-powered, idealistic group of lawyers who valued quality legal work, dedication to clients and a no-nonsense work ethic, plus a commitment to unpaid pro bono work which every one of our lawyers was expected to do.

As for pro bono legal work, I went back thinking of the Darlene Renner case, which I basically did for free, since I lost the case. We had a contingency fee agreement. No jury award, no fees. That was still very hard to get over. I had recurring episodes of regret.

Then one day a judge in the lower level state District Court called me with a request. Would I consider working a day or two as a "pro-tem judge" in the small claims/traffic/misdemeanor court because a regular judge needed a lawyer to fill in? This common practice of using experienced trial lawyers to substitute for judges on a short-term basis never included women lawyers that I could remember. I eagerly agreed. After a short training session, I periodically came to the court, donned a robe and became "judge for a day."

I enjoyed the challenge to my legal knowledge and pressure to decide issues, as well as efficiently manage the docket and court room. Although the pro-tem judge experience involved low level traffic and misdemeanor cases, my appetite for judicial work bubbled up in me.

The energy fired up my busy trial practice, while I occasionally dreamed of someday becoming a Superior Court judge. Since all current trial court judges were fully engaged with no inkling of retirements on the horizon, my fantasies of a judicial position dried up in the back shelves of my mind. Carrying on with my fulfilling legal work at the firm forced me to put aside my fascination with the idea of a judicial position.

I was voted in as a junior partner, relishing the status and my participation in minor firm management duties. My new title helped with client development as well. I felt stable and in sync with my goals and aspirations.

Busy with the work I loved, it never occurred to me to seriously consider running for the judiciary. Most new judges were appointed by the governor when a vacancy occurred, then ran as an incumbent in the next election—a huge advantage I did not have because of zero connections to the sitting governor. Judges rarely retired on a time line that would allow for open filing by interested candidates. An open judicial slot scenario was totally outside my radar.

Chapter 22

Roller Coaster Ride: Court of Appeals

SPRING WAS IN FULL BLOOM WHEN I GOT SUCKED into filing as a candidate for Washington state Court of Appeals Judge in 1993. I guess sucked in is not quite accurate, since I was a willing participant all the way. It started with a longtime Court of Appeals judge who announced his retirement, leaving a vacancy for an open slot before the election cycle began.

The Honorable George Whitten called me to discuss my possible interest in filing for his upcoming judicial vacancy. I was stunned, then flattered. Judge Whitten and I talked a few times after that initial call. He persisted in his encouragement for me to become the first woman Court of Appeals judge in Division Three, which included all of eastern Washington as part of the Washington state court system. I had handled multiple cases before him while he was a Superior Court judge, and had argued appellate cases at the Court of Appeals after he was appointed. He had capped off an outstanding judicial career. Judge Whitten knew my background as a federal prosecutor, a private practice trial lawyer, plus my activism in professional and civic organizations. He said I would be "perfect for the job."

"You have the maturity, plus broad experience in criminal and civil trials, both federal and state courts at multiple levels. Your involvement in professional and local service organizations will help. Perfect resume."

"It takes a lot more than a resume," I replied.

My professional world consisted of trial lawyering and in overall terms, problem-solving as an advocate for those in legal jeopardy. My comfort level rested on my confidence in this worthwhile role that was now familiar to me.

Sure, I had a resume, but I doubted my readiness for a huge challenge like Court of Appeals judge. However, my wild imagination of a path to the Court of Appeals made me an attentive listener. Judge Whitten offered to take me under his wing. We met in his office to talk more.

"Diana, I believe many of my judicial colleagues would endorse you. They know your reputation and have seen you in both trial and appellate court."

"The idea sounds both daring and daunting." I became breathless in the moment.

"Take a while and think it over. Talk with your family, colleagues and friends who know you well." His sincerity was persuasive. I bathed in the glow of his compliments and offers of assistance.

"Well, I need time to take this all in."

"Not too much time. Filing deadline is May 12. My retirement date creates an open judicial slot which could attract other candidates," he said.

Judge Whitten and I shook hands. I thanked him

again, and left his office chambers with a full load of excitement and trepidation.

After my conversations with Judge Whitten, my thoughts grew serious about running for the Court of Appeals, considering the prestige of the office and the first woman thing. I imagined the approval of my family and law partners. Then there was the job itself.

As a Court of Appeals Judge, I would review appeals of court rulings from trial court cases. This definitely intrigued me. Research in case law and its interpretation was the Court's main focus. By that time as an experienced trial lawyer, I assigned basic legal research to our firm's interns and associates who did trial prep tasks. I loved my work as trial lawyer editing interns' trial briefs, where I evaluated the accuracy and weight of legal arguments, putting on the finishing spin before trial. All of that would fit perfectly with a judge's role at the Court of Appeals.

I recognized my skill not only in analyzing issues and effective advocacy, but also my ability to decide cases as a non-partisan arbiter. Substituting as a pro-tem judge in lower court was now under my belt. I had experience as arbitrator or mediator in cases where the litigants opted out of a trial setting, where case resolution offered a less expensive, informal and efficient process. Decisiveness came naturally to me.

Part of my success as a trial lawyer was my ability to evaluate the pros and cons of the other side of a case—judging risks and benefits. A judicial officer must assess the merits of the parties' positions, and make well-articulated decisions supported by factual evidence and applicable law. Without any particular hubris, I just figured I could do that as a judge. The harder challenge was the campaign, since our state mandated an election process for judges, even if an appointment was made between election cycles.

The next step was talk with my family, my partners and other lawyer colleagues. Almost everyone encouraged me. But I heard words of caution about practical realities from my husband Michael and from some partners in the law firm. Concerns about finances, time demands, stress.

For my family, there would be significant monetary expense, as well as little time for normal family life from May to September, the campaign period. If I survived the primary, the campaign would run into November.

I realized the potential effects on my law firm—fewer billable hours, client anxiety, and certainly lost income for both me and the firm, together with all the distractions of a campaign. I would not ask for a leave of absence, but plan to carry on with my practice "as usual," assuring my partners with what turned out to be a false promise. Obviously, I would need help with my clients and cases. A voice inside me called out chilly warnings I ignored. I had no idea how hard this would be.

My women lawyer friends were ecstatic and pushed me hard to file for the position. Judge Whitten persuaded other judges to endorse me. Things moved fast and I felt the roller coaster ride, as I slid into the "candidate" role. I dwelled on all the positives, my go-to attitude.

Josie, my best friend lawyer, offered herself up as my campaign manager. She assured me she knew lots about the political machinations of running for judge. I suppose she made that up, but I trusted her as my heartfelt confidant and political animal with boundless energy. She had an unlimited ability to organize efficiently. I know she didn't sleep much. Perhaps her habit of little sleep was her secret weapon. I welcomed her unquestioning support and affection.

Since the judicial post was an elected position, it was necessary to file officially, together with a $1,000 filing fee. I needed a campaign treasurer. My close friend Jason Brent, C.P.A., generously volunteered for the job. He opened a campaign account, set up the books and took care of requiring financial filings. The Code of Judicial Conduct would govern the campaign activities.

When I leaped out as a candidate, things happened fast. I hired a pricey public relations firm for advertising and publicity. They scheduled press coverage for my formal candidacy announcement event at the front entry of the law school. The state Bar Association Judicial Evaluation committee interviewed, evaluated and rated me "Well Qualified." The labor-intensive process of design and production of campaign materials went into full gear.

Former law school classmates and friends, plus two of my law firm partners formed part of the "Diana Keatts Campaign Committee." The committee also included my two married daughters and my loyal legal assistant Dawn. We met twice a week in early morning hours in the firm's conference room to strategize and review assignments.

The time and effort to get the campaign organized and moving was staggering. A few of my law partners began to fade away from me, distant and less enthusiastic about the process. Both Dawn and I tried to minimize office time spent on the campaign, but it was inevitable that our productivity for the firm's practice and clients diminished significantly. Supportive partners stepped in with help for my pending cases. I negotiated with various opposing counsel and the court for trial continuances where possible. Many clients showed understanding, and a few helped with the campaign.

Michael, my low-profile husband, didn't like a public fuss. He preferred anonymity in the background.

"I'll organize some guys to make yard signs in Dad's garage," he said. "But don't expect me to show up at your public appearances or those campaign events, county fairs, neighborhood coffees. You know, all that stuff Josie arranges for you."

"I know. I love you, sweetheart. We'll have yard signs all over Spokane and eastern Washington."

I hugged him again and again. To do all this for me warmed my heart and reaffirmed his generous love. He had a lot to put up with and I knew it wasn't easy. Especially the thousands of dollars we loaned to the campaign fund, unlikely to ever be paid back. Michael got friends and family to support me. He also arranged work sessions at my father-in-law's garage, with a table saw, tools and all things necessary for an assembly line. They made hundreds, maybe thousands of those signs.

Our son and wife came from out of town to help with signs and door belling.

My legal assistant Dawn was a tall, blond, brash, formidable woman who worked tirelessly on my campaign. Strikingly attractive, she often wore flashy clothes, demanding attention with her energetic competence. Standing up, having conversations with our office lawyers forced them to physically look up to her—I doubt they liked that. She spoke her mind and we clicked. In my legal practice, she produced mountains of support work with incredible ease. We were a smooth compatible team.

I often realized Dawn could probably do most of my job independently, with her quick intelligence, instincts and knowledge. She drafted letters, routine pleadings, and knew the rules of civil procedure with their practical applications. She would do anything for me. I felt the same about her.

Dawn had needs I recognized but could not always fulfill. With her young twin daughters and an unpredictable husband whose framing business was financially vulnerable, she often worried about money. Many times, I had unsuccessful discussions with my partners about my recommended extra salary raises for Dawn in line with her value and accomplishments, including billable hours that demonstrably benefitted the firm. I personally gave her small cash bonuses under the table for particular jobs well done, but felt that was never enough to relieve Dawn's concerns about family finances.

One early morning campaign meeting, we were

talking logistics of campaign signs. Where to put them, how to attract attention in specific locations, the best ways to organize the task force going door-to-door asking people to post yard signs. Spokane was a sign town. Election cycles brought out the signs, in businesses, apartment windows, yards, and banners on public busses. One committee member mentioned the trend in local political campaigns for supporters to stand on busy street corners holding up signs and waving as motorists drove by. I didn't think that would be appropriate for me or anyone else to sink to that depth of desperation in a judicial campaign. Before I could comment on the issue, my assistant Dawn had a question.

"Oh Diana, will I have to stand on street corners waving your signs?"

"No, no, Dawn. I won't do that. Not for a judicial campaign. But no doubt you'd attract a lot of attention."

She looked relieved, and gave her broad Julia Roberts' smile. She would have perched herself on any street corner for me. She was that dedicated.

After I filed for the judicial slot, the campaign evolved into a nonstop parade of activities, including personal appearances at organization meetings, informal coffees, and fund-raising gatherings. As a judicial candidate, I could not raise funds myself. I would speak and answer questions, then leave the gathering and my campaign manager Josie would solicit for campaign contributions. We received many small donations and a few large ones from close friends and family.

The campaign roared on with speeches, TV

appearances, photo-ops, interviews and newspaper articles. Everywhere I went, at the office, in court, on the street, I was a candidate who had to be "on." I carried extra pantyhose and makeup in my briefcase to ensure that I didn't scurry around with a run in my hose or without proper eyeliner. In my dreams I had embarrassing visions of pantyhose springing out of my briefcase pocket in court or at a deposition.

Of course, my partners expected me to continue earning income for the firm. My busy trial practice churned on, as Dawn and I strained to keep up. She was a multi-tasker, and tolerated the chaos better than I. She was good at keeping a low profile in her cubicle while doing campaign work when she should have been doing legal work for the firm. My partners knew what was going on, so they ignored Dawn most of the time. They just wanted the election to be over.

After I filed for the open judicial slot, three others filed. One was the county prosecuting attorney who had been in office for over 25 years, having won many elections. The second filer was a sitting Superior Court judge with a high profile. These two men had plenty of name recognition going for them. The fourth candidate was a former Court of Appeals clerk now in private practice. These three men were intimidating competition.

I figured I had some advantage being the first and only woman candidate. I emphasized my breadth of legal experience, as judicial candidates were precluded from making "platform" speeches by the Code of Judicial Conduct. Then my inexperience as a candidate tripped me up.

I thoughtlessly attended a political rally for a county assessor candidate one evening. Thoughtlessly, because my friend the candidate was a Democrat seeking a partisan office. It did not occur to me that the partisan issue posed a problem. I attended primarily to show support for my friend, and incidentally to mingle with like-minded acquaintances.

The campaign manager of one opponent, the sitting Superior Court judge, called Josie the next day to report that I was seen at the assessor candidate's election rally. The campaign manager threatened to send a letter to the Elections Commission notifying them of my ethical violation because of attendance at a partisan political event. Josie rushed to my office and closed the door abruptly.

"Diana, this could be serious."

"God, I feel like an incompetent moron." I shook my head in total distress.

"I'm trying to think of a way out. This should not be the big deal that he's making of it. I know this guy, the campaign manager. We've had a case together, on opposite sides. He's pretty obnoxious. Likes to intimidate people. He's trying to undermine you."

Josie sat there fidgeting. We were both out of sorts. Josie then straightened up and changed the subject.

"Diana, you have the panel discussion before the Bar Association tomorrow morning. You have to focus and get prepared. You need to march in there and show them what you're made of."

I sat there, feeling numb and empty. I mumbled, "But I'll be sweating out this stupidity of mine. What can we do?"

"Look, let me handle it. I've worked with this campaign manager dude before. I'll try to persuade the asshole to simmer down and get real. Put it out of your mind for now. I'll check in with you later."

I gave her a big hug, and tried to breathe.

Josie was a savvy negotiator. She managed to convince the campaign manager to direct the critical letter to me only, without involving the Elections Commission. That put my violation "on the record" in a threatening way without official action. If the Commission had been notified formally, the press may have gotten wind of it and had a field day. I would have been deeply humiliated, looking foolish and incompetent. Perhaps cited for a violation of judicial ethics. Josie totally saved me.

"Josie, you are sent from heaven. I owe you big time."

I felt so relieved, and came close to tears. Josie had rescued me from my own stupidity. I hugged her tight, and thanked her again and again.

She was tough, yet her soft side often helped her in tight situations. She always gave me helpful advice and cautionary instructions. After my faux pas, Josie kept flawless track of my every move in the campaign. I felt so grateful for my guardian angel, but still felt like an idiot and doubted my own competence.

The grueling campaign continued, seeming more like four years instead of the four months moving toward the primary election. I never imagined a campaign would be so demanding. If I survived the primary as one of the two top vote getters, I would go on to the November general election. Each day hyped up my mixed feelings of unchecked excitement and repressed anxiety.

I was aware that a win would require another two months of brutal campaigning, but I was so overcome with my own importance as a Court of Appeals candidate, none of that sank in. I anticipated a big victory, and my ego craved the attention. Nothing else mattered. Outlines of a celebration speech whirled around in my head.

The day of the primary election finally arrived, with our home full of supporters that evening. Everyone felt expectant and hopeful, after what we had accomplished during the past months. Our dining room table was overloaded with homemade food, set up before I arrived. We ate, drank and laughed ourselves silly, remembering incidents during the campaign. I couldn't thank people enough. Feelings of gratitude and camaraderie overwhelmed me.

Two television sets monitored the election results. At first, when results from some counties within the Court of Appeals boundaries reported in, all four candidates ran about even. One of the counties showed an uptick for me. We all cheered, feeling warm with excitement. As more numbers came in, the prosecutor candidate moved ahead. Then the sitting judge candidate's results rose to a dead heat with the prosecutor. My votes continued to stack up, but at a slower rate than the others. The fourth candidate, former Court of Appeals clerk, ran behind in last place.

The numbers got bleaker for me. We kept a close watch as I fell behind when more counties reported.

The results ran in a pattern—I was stuck in third place and stayed there. Another anxious hour passed. Our festive atmosphere cooled.

Some supporters quietly left the party. Others stood around hugging me and faking their enthusiasm. Michael held me tight in loving silence. By this time, the numbers talked. I was not one of the two top vote-getters to qualify for the general election. I had lost.

After everyone left, Josie and I dropped onto my front porch steps, sitting against each other, trying to prop ourselves up. Our desperate disappointment hung over us on that warm full-moon night.

"You were awesome, Josie," I said through hugs and tears.

"Don't worry, we'll kill them the next time. Whenever that is. This is just a dry run. We made a great showing. Incredible for a first-time candidate."

"I know, I know."

"Running against those two well-known candidates with public personas was a tough hill to climb. The name recognition thing did it for them."

"Yeah."

Sitting there in the dark night air, we resolved to move on after this learning experience. Proud of what we accomplished, we repeated accolades to each other. But it was hard to focus on tomorrow, because that night's pain wouldn't stop.

"I love you, Josie. I can never pay back all you've given me." I couldn't stop hugging her as we sat there in the dark.

Finally, we were silent and just looked up at the moon, thinking about what might have been. And what might be in the future. We were out of words.

I eventually went to bed, feeling deflated, sad and depressed, especially considering the devotion of all my supporters and how I had let them down. I melted into failure, my perfectionist upbeat attitude gone. Michael held me tight. He couldn't sleep either. I knew I had to get up the next morning, put on a fresh face and confront reality. Especially my partners and others in the legal world who would be watching me.

The next morning, I ordered flowers for Josie, put on my best power suit and attacked the day. Michael kept up light banter during breakfast, trying to cheer me up in his knowing way. At the office, I smiled, thanked everyone, tried to be grateful, and act like it was all okay, saying stuff like "Good experience. Maybe next time. Paving the way for others." In my state of mind, it was all bullshit. I had wanted to pave the way for myself. I had been the center of attention, and now nothing.

In the days following the election, I had waves of crying jags as I walked in the park alone. Crankiness became my default emotion. I shut my office door to ward off my partners and employees, even my legal assistant Dawn, though she was hard to ignore. I kept thanking her whenever I could. She was suffering too. Visitors stayed away. People in the office acted distant. I was distant to myself.

How did I get out of it? I don't know. It was gradual. I forced myself to write thank-you notes and make calls to my committee members and supporters. I became a full-time bitch at home, even though I have an underlying sunny disposition. Michael humored me with occasional positive comments and lots of silence. The election loss felt acute because I had fully expected to win.

    I busied myself with loose ends. Things like meeting with my campaign treasurer, making sure the outstanding bills were paid and reporting completed. The campaign had cost almost $50,000. Michael and I were out of pocket for most of it. We sold some of our investments to cover the campaign bills. I felt guilty for wasting our retirement assets. Michael felt the financial loss in a big way, but mostly kept his frustrations to himself. We hadn't realized a campaign would be so expensive.

    My sense of self-pity was mixed with an odd sense of embarrassment. I avoided people and didn't return phone calls. I noticed the bleak sky more than bright curves of cloud formations. My energy lagged. Our social calendar emptied out. Boredom and a sense of futility surrounded me. I sometimes stayed home from the office, sat on our deck with a deepening lack of direction. When I think back now, that time is a blur to me. My spirit needed healing.

    Dawn worried when I didn't show up for work. She got calls from anxious clients wanting to make appointments. My cases, having been postponed during the campaign, moved ahead with assigned trial dates which needed attention. I felt little motivation, but knew I had to get back to work in full force. Yet dragging myself back into the office and courtroom did not inspire me. I kept making excuses.

One day while wasting time ignoring my desk piled up with unfinished work, I stared out the office window at the fall colors in the park below. I got up from my desk and headed down to the park where I walked through tree-lined paths where fall leaves practically blinded me. One of those crystal-clear days where the scarlet, vermilion and honey colors wrap you up and steal your breath away.

Back upstairs in the office restroom, I blinked back a few tears, suddenly wondering what I was running away from. I took a long look in the mirror and told myself out loud to quit feeling sorry for myself. I slapped my cheeks and took several deep breaths. Then went back to my office and opened a file folder to review a pending case.

Later that afternoon, I called Josie. I needed reassurance. We met for lunch the next day. She showed up looking full of energy and alive with enthusiasm. A welcome sign considering my dreary demeanor. I plopped myself down and started in.

"Josie, I have zero motivation. I feel like shit. It's killing me."

I paused to catch my breath.

"But I've got to get out of this funk. Take care of my clients and dig into my cases."

"Well, yes...of course. I completely understand. But, Diana, think about it—you had a spectacular run for Court of Appeals judge. Consider your supporters and all those who endorsed you."

"Yeah, I know."

"Diana, this is the thing. You need to realize the positive effects of the campaign. All that exposure to the public will increase in your client base. People know you. They admire your drive and ambition taking the plunge in the campaign."

"Well yeah, I've had new client calls. But haven't taken advantage of them."

"You'd better get with it soon, or you'll lose the momentum." Her direct gaze made me feel ashamed of my prolonged self-pity.

"Josie, you always give me kick starts. Sometimes in the butt. Which I need now."

I don't know what it was that brought me back. I just felt so dark and defeated that there was nowhere else to go. Josie insisted bluntly that I knock it off and quit feeling sorry for myself.

"It's your own choice about whether or not you're defeated." We talked on and on.

"Find a way back and make your life matter. You've always thought that way."

Hearing her insistent words, I could feel a spark light up my familiar energy. From there my inner fire began to flare. She could have been a clinical psychologist.

We sat a while longer, as she told me of her expanding law practice and possibly hiring an associate to help with her increasing case load. She had huge demands and massive stress during the time-consuming campaign. I knew it must have affected her ability to keep up. Now she was digging in. I needed to do the same.

I somehow plunged in to catch up, and gradually accepted new clients. My familiar routines and habits clicked in, even though I still felt bouts of regret. The campaign contacts and referrals piled up. Too many to handle by myself. We hired another associate to take over some of the load. Dawn, back in her stride, continued as invaluable as ever. We spent long hours and had many successes for our clients. Some of my partners, distant during the campaign, warmed up. Spending 110% of my time earning fees for the firm helped, since billable hours ruled in senior partners' minds.

As I returned to the legal work of solving problems and negotiating solutions, I argued, fought, and mostly won cases for clients. I felt a new dimension to my professional life, more integrated with a sense of direction. I volunteered for pro bono cases, which brought satisfaction to me and my indigent clients.

Although the roller coaster ride campaign uplifted me with self-centered adulation, the crash of losing the election drove me through hell. I moved from simplistic narcissism into necessary realization of my limits. The wild ride and later descent into self-pity gave me balance that clarified my vision. Losing big took me on a dark journey that ironically resulted in a deeper understanding of the complexities of success.

Only then did I own my whole self, which meant appreciation of my inner power to help others, to live a life that matters, and build a legacy for women lawyers who would follow me.

Author's Afterword

The Girl Left Behind: Leaving Footprints

When I became a lawyer, I didn't set out to break barriers. Thoughts and dreams of my life's work didn't imagine appointment as a federal prosecutor, entry into an all-male law firm as a trial lawyer, and becoming the first woman partner. Yet I didn't perceive these as abnormal roles, even though I never met a woman lawyer before I started law school.

Becoming a lawyer just fit in with what I liked. As a child, I was fascinated with words and word games, things like crosswords and Scrabble. I read voraciously and wrote for the fun of it—stories, poems, book reports, newsletter articles for the school paper. Writing forced me to think logically, though much of what I wrote was fantasy. The speech competitions and spelling bees in my youth raised my competitive juices and increased my vocabulary. I liked deciding things for myself and taking charge.

My parents recognized that I preferred arguing to polite conversation. I wasn't a debater until high school, but often dived into unpopular sides of issues. Taking the other side of a discussion for argument's sake was something I couldn't resist. That renegade habit drew criticism from fussy teachers. My favorite teachers tolerated my attraction to the dissent, debating issues from a different point of view.

Luck was with me along the way. I leaned on classmates, professors, employers and lawyers who offered advice and counsel as my idea of a law career captivated my imagination. My generous supportive husband and children were the ears that listened and the arms that surrounded me with never-ending love and confidence. They were caring anchors who kept me balanced, especially when I needed reality checks of my high-flying obsessions.

During my law career, I became an enthusiastic mentor, despite being a bit self-conscious about that role. I didn't have all the answers, and was embarrassed to disclose my egregious mistakes and miscalculations in struggles as a new woman lawyer. In doing so, mentoring became a learning process for me as well. I was in a unique position to share the highs and lows of my experience. To tell others what mattered to me. To show people that women lawyers in any field can make a huge difference in others' lives, even in the face of society's deep cultural bias of rewarding men for power plays and behaviors in and out of the courtroom that women lawyers are expected to avoid.

My opportunity to mentor began in the U.S. Attorney's office. Reflecting on the bright energetic women interns, I am impressed and proud of their later accomplishments. Cynthia was appointed U.S. Magistrate after lawyering at a top-notch law firm. Maryanne became an Administrative Law Judge. After law school, Penny from Alaska worked for and later became the Director of a public interest law firm serving native Americans. She also taught as a law professor. A trial lawyer in her first job, Petra followed my lead eventually as a federal prosecutor. Now she shines as a role model for today's interns in the federal enclave where I began my journey.

In my later private practice, I had the privilege to mentor several outstanding women with career experience who were actively considering whether to enroll in law school. Ruth Ann was a high-profile corporate consultant who desired to broaden her opportunities with hospital clients in a field undergoing major structural and management changes. Suzanne, a competitive golf professional, wanted to move into the expanding field of sports law. Kathleen had pursued a mostly unsuccessful acting career, and decided to change directions. Divorced with two young daughters, she overcame tremendous odds, graduated at the top of her law school class, joined a prestigious Seattle law firm, and later became a District Court judge. Now partly retired, she directs plays in local civic theatre, her first love. All of these amazing women thrived in their chosen leadership roles after completing law school.

The rocky path I traveled as a woman lawyer "in the day" uniquely positioned me to help others. My most gratifying moments made me realize that my own history and advice moved other women in their journeys through law school and beyond. I view their progress with a long lens, realizing that mentoring is a necessary process that must continue.

My own adventures along the way produced many oddities, like being called the "girl lawyer" in the all-male prosecutor's office. I hated that demeaning label. Of course, the men were never called "boy lawyers." Reflecting back, I wonder if some saw it as a harmless pejorative term, relating to my path toward maturity as a full-fledged lawyer. I did not see it that way. It was a clear putdown of my feminine gender. I still shudder about starting a law career at age 38—or any age—as the designated "girl lawyer."

Substantive battles as a trial lawyer in the trenches sapped my energy while my spirit absorbed purpose and meaning. In those times, written reflections of mind and heart were necessarily postponed. Later realizations gradually percolated to the surface, along with an understanding of the role I played as pioneer, explorer, warrior, and the "girl lawyer" label I left behind.

Decades later, women lawyers inhabit their professional lives with confidence in the company of others like themselves. They expect to be known simply as lawyers, judges, professors, prosecutors, defenders—without the excess baggage of earlier days. These lawyers followed footprints, and more importantly, leave their own prints for lawyers of the future. I dedicate this creative work to their successful progress.

Acknowledgements

First of all, thanks to my parents and to my husband Larry. I wish they had lived to see the publication of this book.

Thanks to my publisher, Luminare Press, Patricia Marshall and her talented team, especially Kim Harper-Kennedy and Melissa Thomas for their exceptional expertise in bringing my manuscript to publication.

I owe thanks beyond measure to David A. Oas, author, filmmaker, professor and extraordinary human being, for his insights, endless copy editing, colorful advice and belief in my book, which inspired me to complete this decades-long writing adventure.

I am grateful for the time, attention and constructive comments of copy editors Anne Bellegia, Lucia Smith and granddaughter Katelyn, as well as my three children, Cynthia, James and Pamela, who listened affectionately and offered valuable suggestions.

Thanks also to my critique writing group, especially Elizabeth Hallett and Trish Broersma, and my Southern Oregon University/OLLI writing class members, all of whom cheered me on with their helpful encouragement.

I gained thoughtful reflections from numerous writers about women in the law, especially personal lifework accounts by women lawyers, including those of intellectual pioneers at the Supreme Court: Justice Ruth Bader Ginsburg, Justice Sandra Day O'Connor and Justice Sonia Sotomayor.

I have aspired to present a wide spectrum of experiences in this fictionalized work by describing actual lawyers, prosecutors, lawsuits and more in the milieu of the times as they affected women lawyers, but also to relate those experiences to larger political and cultural questions. Any resemblances to persons living or dead is purely coincidental.

Made in the USA
Monee, IL
29 January 2020